ENGAGING CATTLE

AN AMEN CORNER OF PHANTASMAGORICAL TALES

KEN POYNER

Barking Moose Press, LLC
Dare to read dangerously

Acknowledgement is provided to the following magazines or collections in which the listed items below first appeared:

Allegory Why Do You Do It

Blotterature A Thought Process, Necessary Work

Café Irreal Lover's Art, The Growing Compromise

Corium Rivals

Crack the Spine Appetite

Danse Macabre Cultural Bias, The Liberator, The Night Before, The Particularly Able Agent, Trading Crafts

Dream City Blues The Next Colony

Everyday Fiction Word Crime

Five Hundred Miles Comfort

Flash Fiction The Measure

Foliate Oak Consequences

Freshwater Review Return

Gone Lawn Migration's End, The Public Decency

In-Between Altered States The Rescue

Mind Candy The Quest for Fidelity

Mobius The Agitation

Open The Triumphant Stroll

Potato Soup Journal Stalkers

RDP Society The Gift

Red Dirt Forum Ruling Party

Riverbabble Between Seasons, In Sympathy, The Curious Commitment

Runcible Spoon The Costume

Rune Bear Community Evolved

TABLE OF CONTENTS

THE PARTICULARLY ABLE AGENT

Heed well, my fellow contrarians.

This new agent has only been on the job for the last month and a half, and already he is doing as well as a year's seasoned veteran. He made quota for just his third week at the job, and exceeded the next week's target by ten percent. Quite some doing, given the outrageous and unreachable quotas the Bureau intentionally sets. His superiors are taking notice. There is talk already of his being quietly moved to a more fertile district, one where he can spread his talents liberally into more dark corners and rounds.

No one likes to say it about so new a man, but he appears to be going places. He seems to have the knack.

It is not that he works much harder than his mates. Oh, he puts in a goodly amount of effort; but, like anyone, he wants to maximize his take-home prize while conserving his involvement. The real danger lies in the principle angles of his imagination.

It was he who thought of swimming pools. Yes, someone else would have come up with the idea sooner or later - but he hit on the find almost as soon as he had his dot-collection ledger. Hotels that have an international clientele mark their swimming pools at the shallow and deep end in both English and metric depths, and seldom are both markings in whole numbers. Three feet is zero point nine meters. That stranded decimal is available to be harvested by the roving dot collectors. Pull out the dot, scoot the nine a little to the left, and the zero point nine has become zero nine, and into the dot collector's bin goes the dot.

Five feet is one point five meters, and so, if the pool is internationally marked, there is yet another dot. One point five is rendered one five, and a captured dot.

For a while, only he was collecting these pool dots; but word of good hunting gets quickly around, and, for all he did to hold the lucrative secret, someone followed him or recognized the reason some of his dots were damp or simply imagined his method from his success, and the new class of collection got out. Dot collectors showed up everywhere, a copy of the Dot Collection Ordinance folded into the gray, official Ordinance presentation leather case, and away with the dots they went. From the large resort hotels, to roadside over-nights that had pools inelegantly jammed into their parking lots - all have been relieved of their dots, or are in the process of being inspected for non-whole number depth markings and the accompanying presence of dots.

It was, at first, surprising that it might be the relatively new worker who came up with this bumper unharvested location. After the Ordinance was passed and the Bureau of Dot Removal was ruefully yet efficiently configured, new ideas were fast and direct. One zero zero dot zero zero became one zero zero zero zero. A hundred dollars could be mistaken for ten thousand, if one did not remember to adjust for the transmogrified ordinal spacing. St dot became mere St. Sentences became distinguished not by their endings, but by the capitalization of their beginnings. The many places where a dot might hide were catalogued, and soon after the more long-winded planning discussion of their effective collection began.

Yes, a new idea is comparatively rare – in part, no doubt, because there are so many known forests of available dots that prides of agent dot collectors concentrate on the details of gathering all the members in any one class, instead of moving from diverse target to diverse target – interested in the plenitude targets to event blindness, working towards the total extinguishment of some specific species of dot.

Given the agents' laser-focus, it is surprising that the dots in this threat-notice yet survive. They could be overlooked in a general, all-encompassing cull – but, with some collection agents purely focused on collecting the end of sentences, we have had to take our practiced Herculean evasive measures in order to keep our warning sentences properly ended. We have to spirit our notices and effects, make invisible our charters and minutes, become ghosts when we faithfully document our resistance.

So, in this notice, we herewith raise the alarm for this new, chillingly effective, dot collector. In even his short career, he has exceeded his quota too often. He has plans and recognition and imagination, and his outcomes eventually are shared, willingly or not, with other practitioners of his ridiculous craft. Given time, he will at least marginally improve the entire greedy workforce of dot collection agents, possibly think his way into the Means and Methods division, gain a warm place for the unabated breadth of his fancy.

Who knows? Perhaps it might be he who finds a logic to seal the so far unaccepted argument that commas are simply lazy periods, thus ersatz dots, and thus should be gathered under the anti-dot ordinance. Perhaps he will imagine a mathematical proof that a hyphen is a time-shifted dot, or a dot with a slur – who could suffer such coiled thinking? - but an imagination such as his might bend the matter of the logic around. We have cause to think he is special. We have cause to think he is an evolution.

He must be stopped. We must write of him a short and ended history. He must be the target of our efforts to maintain the dots remaining amongst us. He must be done.

Period.

THE BENEDICTION

"Is it time now?" asked Ecru as she crouched, her hands and knees beneath her, her head pushed forward in the tall grass, watching the village between the reeds.

Lying flat on his stomach, chin on the ground, aware of the village but not watching it, Brown replied, "No, I will tell you when it is time. You follow. You help with the gathering. Remember: follow."

Brown wished that Ecru would unwind herself. A girl of fourteen on her first gathering, she was not yet able to surround what she was becoming, could not wrap sensuously about the space she was growing into. Her progress, yet lack of finish, was evident to everyone except herself, though within the coming year the expectations of her village would match puzzle-piece with her own and a new physics would take spark.

They and the others were in the tall unbowed grass, but only a few yards from where it grew flat and trampled. The edge of any village always smells of playfully near things: of the evening's fresh cooking once removed; of a dog not unlike the neighbor's; of children playing too far from the narrow paths between comfortable buildings; of the untamed prey that wanders as close as it drearily can, until it cannot stand the enlarging smell of civilization any longer and shies back into the deep.

The raiding party heartily counted the whipping red, orange and yellow streamers. There were more than many members in the raiding party had learned to acknowledge. Atop short poles they flowed from their moorings; ribboned by the wind; in the rare moments of calm, touching the sacred ground beneath them; or wrapping back onto their poles and sliding lazily against the hand smoothed outer finish.

Lights were going out in the village: candles here, lanterns there, the few electric beacons lasting longer, but seeming themselves to grow ever wearier.

Ecru knew that Brown, having himself gone on half a dozen raids, would be a good teacher. He would see that she went to the right spot, waited for the right signal, applied herself as though she were just one limb of this exercised animal. He would do that part of the thinking, for which she would be the stinging execution.

From her knot in the grass, she could see one member of their party crawl crab-like out onto the flattened grass. Another followed him half a body length later. They edged on hands and knees, backs swayed into spoons, the side-to-side motion of their hips exaggerated to keep their rear-ends from rising too high in the thickening dark.

Quiet and stealth make for a raid: force is not our way. Ecru spoke to herself the mantra that Black had made her learn before she was ever put up for selection into a raiding party. She liked the feel of it on her lips, the taste of it across the blood between her teeth: so she moved respectfully the whole bounty of her mouth even when she spoke the mantra without putting breath behind it.

Brown looked without shine over to her and said, "Stay on my hip. Always stay on my hip. Do not get ahead of me!"

And slowly off he started. She breathed twice more and followed, trying to sidle like a crab, trying to keep that unruly bum of hers down. She snaked inside her clothes as she has seen her mother snake for her father once the children were turned out to bed. She felt an electric smoothness she imagined to be akin to the glowing power that her mother must feel at those caprices of cloth folding and bunching and being less tactful than the body beneath.

The first man reached the first pole and stood jackstraw straight up. Out with his knife and, snip, snip, the first flag was down. The man who had been on his hip stood at the second pole and, snip, snip, the second flag came down. Soon, men and women were converging on all the poles and, snip, snip, the flags came down. Ecru reached the slaughter herself and made a furious bowl of her arms. Men and women came to her, folding the flags as best they could, placing them across the rack she made between elbow and fingers. She tried to twist in the direction of the fellow villager coming next, but Brown told her to stand still, to wait for the raiders to come to her, to be the part he needed her to be.

She was not the only one being piled with flags. All the younger raiders were standing like statues, stationed along the edges of the field of poles, each being burdened with civilizations of flags: each being covered with flag after flag – but not with so many that they could not run if they had to. Black had told them all the logistics of this: cutter to holder, and only so much to a holder, so that fully burdened the holder could yet bolt, could take the lead given by a good warning and make a bottomless break for it.

Ecru tried to breathe in when a cutter approached her, tried to breathe out as a cutter left. At times, she took too many breaths, at times not enough. She would think later on how best to breathe. Her chest and diaphragm had to speak more of coordination, but there would be more. Breathing now was only a part of being in service.

A light sputtered dutifully on in the village, and then shortly another. There was a small, wide open face at a far away window and one of the raiders yelled "Away!" and they were running, all of them, no thought of stealth, all first into the tall grass and then soon into the forest and they could hear the robbed villagers stirring and cursing behind them: but no one would chase a raider at night into the forest.

Ecru felt the fuel of the cloth across both of her arms. She felt a warmth she could not place as Brown came up beside her and supported one elbow. They walked now, walked towards the river that would accompany them the rest of the way home. Brown murmured something to her and she thought for a moment this might be her woman-night, but he made no ritual motions: there was no cooing, nor the rain barrel thoroughness of stray stoking, and soon they were at the moon-race of water that fingered their village and provided them the bearings of life.

The water barely moved. This was the still season, the time between the water's rush in and the water's rush out. Brown took a banner from Ecru's arms, and soon others were there to take banners. Each raider bent at the edge of the river and drove a flag into the water, rubbing the cloth against itself, washing the prayers of the former owners out of the pregnant flags, and watching those misshapen enemy prayers lazily float for a while in the life-giving water: then sink like the scat of lost animals into the bed against which the river comforts itself.

One saddle-skinned man, who had been washing more vigorously than most, stood and said, "These now are our prayer flags. The cruel prayers of our rival village are gone. They have been given to the river, who will never release them to God. We can return home and fill these fresh, sterilized flags with our prayers, place them on our poles, and be the one village to know God's crystal, shimmering answers." He moved his arms about like a man putting out feed for the family's chickens, mechanical but sure, and he cooed these well-known lines like a mother putting a colicky child to bed. Ecru knew he had not missed a word. She fumbled to find some error, some missed intonation, but none was there, and the sound of his benediction drifted over the river like mornings of mist and finely kissed fog.

These flags would rise alongside those already hoisted in their village, fattened with their new prayers: with supplications for success, with desires for health, with the need for a rival's pratfall. Ecru might have her own flag, roiled through and through with the wish for a man with a blind heart and fingers that curled thoughtlessly inward when he stood unaware. Hers would be one of a mighty army of many-colored prayer flags that God could enjoy, each whipping out its cautiously wrapped words without the competition and noise of the other villages' prayers, without their petty pleadings and hunger for forgiveness, their shortcomings and ferocities; without their lust for God's limited time.

Everyone strung a prayer flag over his or her shoulders, and when there were not enough for everyone, it was the novice raiders who were left short. They would have to fashion their own prayer flags out of homespun cloth and stolen thread when they returned to their welcoming village. Ecru fell into line behind Brown, who had paid no notice to her since relieving her of a prayer flag. She tried to step into his footsteps, but the dark dazzled her and when she thought she was not in his stride, she was; and when she thought she was in his stride, she was not.

Once, when almost out of the forest, they all heard a rustle going past to the East, coming from the dark at the end of which their village waited. Perhaps it was a coven of fox, or a nest of wolves, or some gathering of prey pulling itself together at the noise of the returning raiding party. Ecru would have liked to have known, but she squatted with the others, waiting in her unknowing for the uncompromising sound - so like a purposed army of tarnished, thieving feet - to devoutly pass and drift away, replaced almost immediately by what soon seemed a nervously rising, stunned lamentation stabbing out a while ahead from the hollowed heart of home.

THE NEXT COLONY

I wanted you to know first thing that I got my emigration papers yesterday. I am the luckiest citizen in the whole stuffed building! I thought I would never get a chance to get off of this rock. It seems they have recently finished the terra prep on a planet called Lenore 5. Somewhere out on some galactic arm or another. I don't even remember reading about them finding it. I look for notice of new discoveries all the time, but I guess the notices are easy to miss. But the emigration permit said that all the pre-fabricated materials, all the start-up supplies, all the pieces and parts we need to assemble new lives, have been delivered and are waiting for willing hands; and the planet's sustainability index has been confirmed - three times, by three separate governments – as wonderfully high: all we have to do is go there and enjoy full employ-ment, luxuriate in prosperity, and drink in the clear skies.

No, I will not miss Earth. Some people, when told they can never come back - that the jump is entirely one way – why, some people hesitate. Whatever for? I guess some think of family here; or their dingy, stunted routines; or imagined connections to imagined landscapes. Perhaps their cherished connection to history — or what we are told is history. I won't miss it. Earth is dirty and crowded and regulated, and all the time it is people, people, people. I am always seeing the back of some stray citizen's head. We live constantly on view, and constantly I cannot help but be the viewer of others. On Lenore 5, we will be able to adjust our schedules to suit ourselves, set our sleep cycles by the coming and going of the light, not by the lottery of slots in sleep hostels. First thing I want to do is run in a straight line. Seems odd, perhaps, but how many straight lines are there on Earth? How many years since anyone has been able to run in a straight line on this dingy, hopelessly cluttered planet? Too many people, too many things, too many compromises. Too much construction to have room to tear down last season's construction. And, if you could run, you would have to request a breathing filter unit upgrade just to be able to chew in enough air to cover your exertion.

Take as fact: I will not miss Earth. I will not miss always hearing a human voice. Always. Always sharing space with three cycles of strangers. Always being on a clock, on a cycle, on a schedule; always having to move on, to move through, to make way; so someone else can do, for a few seconds, whatever you have been doing, and not - by far - doing long enough. Take your brief turn, get your quota, get your taste, and then go away.

I can remember when they discovered Epsilon 3. I wasn't chosen then. I was too young and my personality matrix had not been settled and properly catalogued. But a number of people I knew were chosen; and they waited day by day as the transport ship for that day came gloriously down, looking just like the transport ship from the day before and the day before that: all those people lining up to claim their place with nothing more in hand than their selection notices. Smiles, and the jostling not so ill-tempered, and people pressing back to front perhaps, but this one time finding it actually pleasant, actually wanted. All day long the transport ship loaded, then at dusk zipped up in a streak of atmosphere into brief orbit; and then out to a point where it could, I'm told, switch to space drive and make that one way fold through the ether to Epsilon 3, the new Eden where it would deposit the colonist, and then be scrapped itself to feed the colonial industry that would immediately begin.

Each ship, looking just like the last ship, looking much like the scavenger vessels that work through our trash – the scavenger scows that stutter up into low orbit, and then fire what cannot be saved on a long arc into the dark between planets. There is something hypnotic about all those ships appearing exactly the same, about the day long loading, about all those souls screaming through the air towards a better life that is just a point somewhere outside of their reckoning. Each ship the exact twin of the one the day before, almost monotonous in its utilitarian symmetry. But this dull exact replication is bound to make disassembling those ships, once they land at the colonial world, much easier; and make it simpler to send out from Earth our preformatted molds to those newly discovered worlds, molds that the colonist will use to drape the salvaged hull of each Ark across, building - by blueprint number - homes and factories and recreation facilities and a much better life than any of them could ever have here.

Yes, it has to take a lot of work and time and material to make so many ships. One can barely hold ten thousand people. Thankfully, there is no luggage, no personal effects. I'm told it will be just a few minutes rocketing to a wrinkle in space, then all is a blur, and we will be orbiting Lenore 5, ready to join all the colonist that dropped out of the ether earlier and have already started building and working and stinging their lungs with untreated, unfiltered air - and enjoying open land again, agog with free-standing water, with seeing clouds that have ends.

Sure, I would like to know how other colonization projects have gone. That whole bit about everything being one way is a little hard to swallow, even if I never want to come back. A shout out containing lessons learned from an earlier colony might be nice: postcards of success, a how-to of what not to do, a treatise on the social etiquette of finally having space. The physicists say that the portal in, once scrambled with our transit, cannot sustain traffic back, of any sort. Either way, I'll take my chances. Earth doesn't want us, and, frankly, I don't want Earth. If mistakes have been made on our new worlds, there is no way to learn from them, with every contact being only one way. We might just make those same mistakes again. But we will do so in open spaces, with clear waters, and with comfortable vapor clouds in the sky instead of gas streams.

I wish you had gotten your notice, too. It would be nice to both experience solitude together, to have available work together, to experience openness together. I think you might have been held back because you did so well on your cyber aptitude test, and got that job over in micro-robotics. I've always envied your employment. It keeps your mind off the constant press. I am sure I would be happier if I had rated employment, but I think I would still be burning to go. You should get your chance. Why, this Lenore 5 discovery practically snuck up on us! You had not heard of it, either? Who knows? They may be already terra prepping the next discovery, and you will get a notice that it is time for you to be off, too. I'm sure you will be selected! But, even if you don't go, as they move people out to these new colonies, crowding has to lessen, the pollution has to thin, the environment has to start responding to the reclamation projects that have been going on now for decades. A less populated Earth is a better Earth for everyone. You agree? I could not agree more.

And one day this one-way limitation will be solved. An improved Earth will hear from its extra-dimensional colonies, and we will be reunited. Imagine it, one history again: a cleaner, more open history, where everyone has space to swing her arms and run in a straight line until the muscles grow giddy with exertion.

But, for now, I'm just glad to be leaving. You can wish me luck, but I have already had my round of luck. I am going! You can have anything out of the little I have been allowed to own; that is, if you can find room for it. Where I am going, I will need none of it. I will be free of the whole damn lot of it. I will need nothing at all. Just a hop and a skip up a ramp, strapping into the hold and I will be gone forever into more freedom than I have ever known! Do not envy me, at least not too much. When we get there and I can find a fistful of free soil, I will plant something in your name. A tree, or a bush, or whatever grows there. And it will be yours, swaying free in a distant star's light, with all the oxygen it can gobble and all the room it needs and being master of the volume it claims. Think of it now and again.

APPETITE

Rolling hills, with the closest structure to the road being the American Legion Hall, its old gravel parking lot spread close between the building and the road. A two-lane laminated path that dips and spins economically off center, rising and falling as little as it legally must between bouts of a poor farm land with its domestic dwellings set as far respectfully back as the abodes of trolls.

Chicken coops are kept out of sight, but they are here, too. In deserts, in high-chested forests, in the trilling mountains and so close to the ocean you can feel the sand and salt in the eggs. Everywhere there are chickens. I know the coops rise in their majestic single stories, alive with the chatter of chickens, the omnibus crackle and slam of egg production, the meticulous reclamation of waste. It is an industry: it takes in, it gives out.

Did you know that all domestic chickens come from the same originally exploited bantam breed? One location on the earth, and all the chickens of our planet, from that small genus of fowl, have grown to cover almost every continent, to ennoble almost every table, to be for many the sole point of ownership over another species.

I've eaten chickens in almost every state. It is what I do.

I have the means to devote myself to this. My wealth was finished years ago and I have my personal keep well in hand. I have no vices, no accomplices, nothing that pokes the red eye of wonder out of the pounding cacophony of my dreams. Every morning all I must do is fire up the Ford, shake the disharmony of the hotel bed from my back and my eager-to-learn limbs, and I am off to the rustic roads, off to find the little unknown places deaf in their fog of line-dreary mornings, unsuccessful so far in their rush to become gentrified suburbs.

Soon enough I'm out thirty yards behind someone's antique collection of a home, holding a prize fistful of poultry. Grant me the nobility of it: I eat it all except the beak and feet and bone and large feathers. Oh yes, I can eat the small feathers now.

Just one chicken at each poaching is enough. I am no glutton. It will take hours, like sand in a salt mine, of driving: one headlight on early evenings, wipers on top speed if there is the ganglia of drizzle. Then, two hundred miles down the road, my forthright hunger will again start flashing diagrams to the static of my brain. Images of chickens past will gargle in the empty spaces positioned strategically listless in my memory. I will start looking for the hum and vibrantly colored scent of an artfully profitable hunting ground.

So, when you put your chickens to bed tonight, know that I am driving. I keep both hands on the wheel and hum a song you have heard only when you've plugged your finger accidentally into a live electrical socket. Maybe I will not be driving in your state, not even in your country: but likely, some night, I will be within a stone gargoyle's throw of nearby. And on some good for laundry, windy afternoon - with a hint of drizzle in the air and an elfin burnt-out cold beginning to wheeze - you will see outside in the innocent yard more loose familiar feathers rolling about than you are accustomed to; and then you must run, a shotgun blast of expectations, out to your false security of a coop to start counting and calling, calling and counting. The many, many chickens. And, just now, one less.

TWO AR-15s, WITH A GLOCK ON HOLD AWAITING CREDIT CHECK

I am going to miss my GLA meeting. I've been to eight in a row, and I am actually going to miss not being able to go to the next one. There is a lot to be said for these meetings. I never thought I would last, but I keep coming up with reasons to attend. If you think hard enough, you can justify almost anything.

To be honest though, what I will miss is Nancy. Nancy, with her split front dresses split just a bit too far up; or her short shorts far too short; or her jeans maybe a size and a half too close for breathing. Nancy of the right overages and the right under-ages, seeming halfway between penthouse and trailer park: the porridge just right.

I remember most her soft green key-hole tank top - but she has a number of excruciatingly low-cut slipovers; oh, those diaphanous things you can just imagine slithering over her head and for a bare moment catching her hurried hair; and she occasionally wears a button up with not so many buttons buttoned, at least that you count from where they are tucked in, or from where the tails worn outside trail off. She is the only woman in the group, and no one minds when she sets off on her sing-song story again – about how it all started out in a worry over protection and safety, about being secure in her person; but then moved on to establishing space, to making a hole for herself in the scheme of things; and then dominating the moment, being in control, being one-tough-cookie; and then at the end about being in charge. She started out with an unlikely-to-be-effective, matchbook-sized small clip, small caliber, unreliable contraption; and moved on to a real hand gun; and then an over-and-under 12 gauge with a 22 long rifle; and then she finally made the leap to an assault rifle – and, before she joined the group, ended up with six long guns, three carbines, and a dresser drawer of handguns, each in a neat hard-clip case. All the men in the group would shudder, imagining a nine-millimeter recently cleaned, with the clip set flat within business distance, mixed in with her underwear, perhaps caught up in the leg of a striped thong or pinning a racy black bra to the back of the drawer. Would she have white bikini pants, or opt for wild colors? Would she have lacy bras, or ones assembled for industrial duty, fighting the ampleness they inadvertently highlight? Would her semi-automatics shade to heavy steal or aluminum where it could be substituted? Speed loaders for the revolvers in the same drawer?

She regales us nearly every week with tales of target practice. First the targets were set close, and simply became a goal. Hit them, hit them ever closer to the center. Aim and result. Look for the puff of dirt that meant the round had gone into the berm behind, and not over, or slipped uselessly into the grass in front of the backstop. Later, as the targets were moved back and she grew close to proficient, she imagined the targets as being murderers and rapist, thieves and bikers, Mormons and Scientologists, the boy two doors down who always leaves his bicycle in her driveway. Each getting his come-uppance, each getting his just deserves. She tells how she would come home from the range with a trunk full of guns and spent brass and glare at the boy, knowing no matter how big and sassy he got, no matter how many days he went between shaves or how much color he slipped into his public language, she had the better aim, and she would always have the edge.

No one minds her telling the same story time and time again. She gets emotionally into it and starts to wiggle and jiggle and everyone imagines losing spare change in the cracks and crevices she so ably displays. We all sit cross legged and hope she goes on all night. We look at each other and know it will be one more beer at the bar or straight home and the wife suddenly all aglow and the kids told to stay a while in their rooms and watch whatever they like on television. What used to be a night after the range is now a night after the GLA, all with pretty much the same end for the objects of our affections. Nancy drones on and our imaginations twist and turn and the blood reassess its strategic map and goes for the far target, knowing it will settle for the fifty foot minimal distance qualification in an hour or so.

But it is also entertaining to watch some of the less practiced members be forced to tell their stories. Many of these are ex-militia men, hounded into attending the meetings by their wives or mothers, bribed into wasting this time by the prospect of better domestic tranquility. Men who were used to going out weekend after weekend, wearing camouflage and transporting a few thousand rounds and a handful of rifles and short guns in their trunks, to the separatist farm where they drank beer and trained themselves at selecting sides. For two days, three if there were a holiday, they would run about trying to find value in themselves, looking to establish a structure where they personally had some meaning, some mastery, and could imagine themselves able to strive against something: having the metal to bully those who might be less well armed. When the expense got too much, or the yard work too far behind, or the excuses to the less ballistics-inclined relatives got too bizarre, they ended up here. Each week, we get to watch them squirm and come up with a good explanation for attending the meetings. There are almost always new ones each week. They try to sound like they want to be here, and Nancy is sure a reason to show up; but, really, they are having a hard time sinking back into being ordinary men after ordinance has made them feel king of the hill, top of the mountain, master of men like they once were when they used to be unarmed. It is a lot to give up. Any addiction is. Even if you want to give it up — and there are so many side-bar reasons to keep this one. Every story has to skirt the truth.

But this weekend there will be at least 150 vendors at the Pavilion, a new gun show by a group I've never heard of: a name that rolls off any rights defender's tongue, with free parking, and only an $11.00 each day entry fee. Flags and trucks and a battle-space play-place for the children, along with a pre-teens gun gallery. The mentors at GLA hate it when these events come to town. Yes, they might be able to stave off a half-hearted Fourth of July sale at the local gun shop, or even a week long Defenders of Freedom trade-up firearm event. But no one can beat one of these traveling shows. Show up and play your cards right, and you can bypass background checks, actually test out the latest in laser sighting, walk away with a thousand rounds of overloads, or end up with an antique long gun – in working order – alleged to have been used in a shootout by one side or the other of a real conflict.

They start advertising - television, radio and billboard - a month out, and by the week of the show, anybody who wants to be somebody, but otherwise cannot, is humming to go and pick out the means to his – or, now, her – better personhood. These Gun Lovers Anonymous people might be able to keep us coming to dreary meetings when Nancy is rocking and rolling and her important pieces and parts are about to pop free, given that at the time there is no event on the horizon; but I do not see how they think they can compete with a thirty round magazine, a World War One military issue Springfield, or a 50 caliber polymer-handled snub nose.

Heck, if we had a lot of will power, we wouldn't be here in the first place. We all know we get the gun addiction through low self-esteem; we crave the power that a firearm gives us, and which we could not otherwise claim through force of personality, talent, reasoning or self-assurance. Without the gun, we blend in. With the gun, we are masters of all we survey. Those simple, lovely devices become a part of our personalities, part of that which makes each of us the force we believe we are. No group sitting around bedazzled with the curves of a thirty-year-old single mom, half listening to completely made up stories of contrition and new social viability, is going to keep a need for testosterone in check. You have to be who you want to be. You have to be who denying your own shortcomings forces you to be.

I imagine the GLA mentors will wait alone at the door at the top of the stairs leading into our dust-colored-carpeted, bare meeting place: with the metal cheap hotel conference room chairs, and the spotted walls that are not supposed to be spotted, and the HVAC that seems to work only yesterday and tomorrow. They have been watching the advertisements for weeks, knowing what is coming. One of the vendors is bringing a museum-piece howitzer. If anyone shows up at the GLA meeting the night of the show, that misdirected individual will sit there bouncing a leg until the meeting is adjourned early and he or she, like everyone else, pops the clutch over to the Pavilion, probably with an advance-purchased ticket, and an excuse that, hey, the parking is free. We are not going to buy we tell ourselves. But then we calculate that, over a relatively short time, one of these armaments could be cheaper than Viagra. The wife has been banking the saving on ammunition for a few weeks, and it is now our time. A small purchase won't much be missed in the family finances, and we will feel whole for a while again. Soon we will get back to those damned meetings. We promise.

Nancy will probably be at the show. For all the talking it out, for all the admission that it is an addiction, for all the commitment to finding her value and self-esteem elsewhere, she likes the sense of power that having a semi-automatic weapon happily settled across her lap provides. She likes thinking of that boy and his bicycle as being no trouble at all, nope, none whatsoever. She likes keeping us all on edge two ways – watching that wiggle and how it pops a holster on her side back and forth and across, like a boy driving all-in his best sex — and coming up, to her mind, mediocre.

I'm sure I will catch her there sashaying in one of the great fenced-in aisles — idling between a display spread length-wise detailing some handgun's projected lethality; and on the other side of the narrow walkway an advertisement for the latest in home defense, if your home has 40,000 square feet and is assaulted by a crack corps of paramilitary mercenaries. She will exaggerate the angles of her sweet three-buckets rear stuffed into a two-buckets set of jeans, and twist around so, through both a bra and a t-shirt, her half-dollar sized nipples will introduce themselves to the nearest surrounding three-quarters arc of gawkers. She will draw a flat finger across some fortunate vendor's eyelevel-displayed AR-15, her lower lip pulled under her teasing tongue and held in place by two rock-hard reconstructed teeth.

I will not be the only one —out-of-depth GLA member or not — posed expectedly around the honored hall who wants to slip with her behind the stacked excess bleachers, shielded by the bulk hardwood rifle cases, and deftly, defiantly, deafeningly, delightfully pull her glorious trigger. And I bet, bang, when the bullet went off, I'd be ejected, spent, the brass still hot and smoking, and me uncaring whether the next one is already snug in the chamber or not.

NECESSARY WORK

I always knew light was a collection of things: intertwined wavelengths, cohabitating photons. What we think of as a single shaft of light is actually a thousand variations on the theme of light, all gathered in the same space at the same time. It is a unified cacophony of brilliance, a congress of feral glitters.

I've often wondered why it does not burst: why all these wavelengths colliding do not fly out as fractures of light, as filaments escaping at all angles: a starburst.

Even when broken with a prism, the pieces fall out so orderly, so singularly self-composed. There is no emotion at liberation, no sadness at separation. Each element quivers to its own echo, bunched beside its mate: wholesomely ragged when dismembered, when left so dimensionally alone.

I have noticed how the light leaking out of a prism has no warmth. Going in, it is the white, blended light that leaves heat spots irregularly on the floor. Out of the prism, it has switched warmth for color, impact for appreciation.

I have always thought that if I could get inside the light, I could figure the gradients of its mindful marriage, understand its internal chromatics: discover the twilight of how its warmth scurries out. I see what goes into the prism as more astounding than the feckless disharmony that comes out. The key to the union is what transfixes me: the love of light lies less in its togetherness, than in the reason it seeks to be an oleo. Rainbows are for show. They mislead the ill-informed.

So at night I sit up late into evening distending the light. I pry filament from filament, peel back each distinct element. Captured light wraps sensuously around me, pools luridly on my bed, cascades down onto the lowly rug that protects me each morning from the bare, cold floor. Quanta scurry about, set free like metal shavings around a lathe, colicky at times, but cavorting independently at others. I pick and pry, getting with each attempt deeper: singing my workman's song to the massed wavelengths, humming my brazen curiosity to the happily oscillating photons.

Most of my night, it is I in the dark, making progress: unable to see my hands, unable to see where I should shred with my teeth, where I need to peel with the tips of my worshipping fingernails. I feel the light all around me; the light ponding underneath my bed; the light enveloping; the dark holding itself in awe of me. Beneath each layer of discovery, there is another. Energy lies across my shoulders, hums its sexless mating in my lap. I know I pleasure the dark too greatly, but it cannot be helped.

RULING PARTY

Old man Stratem gets out to vote for every election. I've seen him wiggling down the wrinkle of his driveway, and fighting with the door of his old truck in a thunderstorm, his hat brim beaten flat with the rain and his spectacles nearly washed entirely off. But he stood there, fumbling with his keys, counting them out in the flat of his hand and pushing them around with his dripping fingers until he caught the one that fit and finally jerked open the door; then, still bathwater wet, he made it thunderously into the high school gym to cast his ballot.

That day, almost no one else was driven enough to show up. Not much going on in that election, and the weather being so bad. People tend to take their democracy on a sliding scale, except for old man Stratem.

He is very particular about his coiled politics. Very little wiggle room, and not much space for spice. His ideas are pretty much nailed to the wall with one-way iron spikes, and he does not like change. I can imagine those ideas having been hacked into shape, then dried by his fireplace, and put pristine and as make-do as a mail-order bride on the wall beside. Where he doesn't have an opinion, but senses he needs one, he likes to take it from someone who makes a good noise, but does not complicate the matter. Something short, with unchallenging sentences: a lot of sound, a bit of wind, a good storm cloud or two: that carries the issue for him. Too much thinking, he believes, will get anyone twisted around; and someone who isn't watching for the proper signs might end up going in the wrong direction. To his careful consideration, it is best to drop all the side bars and side roads and side shows, and just stick to getting the whole of the matter down to less than a full paragraph. Or better, down to one phrase; or maybe three good words.

Stratem is one of those who have been beaten by the bank, the utility company, the farm bureau, the machinery salesman, and the manager at the feed store — but he doesn't know it. He will outlive his mortgage, and that is enough. He thinks he has done well for himself, and counts himself as being constitutionally in with the Chosen. The common, salt-of-the-earth Chosen, that would be. He is not into fancy. He is as plain as unsalted dirt, and peacock-proud of it. He knows just what sort of people God favors, and that is where his allegiance lies.

If you want his vote, you have to match his politics in each and every particular, down to the cases and examples. Doesn't matter that the office you are running for doesn't have any jurisdiction in the concerns that pepper his day's collection of self-marshalling routines. If you want to be dog catcher, you need to let him know you agree with him on: abortion, gun rights, immigration, creationism, and unions. And on those damned government regulations, even the ones on industries that he doesn't, at this time, know exist. To him, all of those issues are important things to measure when you are picking the local dog catcher. And, since most people don't vote for dog catcher - even if they show up to vote in that particular election - you, as the hopeful future dog catcher in this town with a wealth of stray dogs, need to make sure that you have Stratem's vote in your pocket. So, no matter what the town's people think, the town could easily end up with an elected dog catcher whose main talent is a flair for matching Stratem's vision of just about everything in the world.

I've watched old Stratem walk into the polling place with his storied gray, thumb-worn and crumpled, piece of paper seemingly asleep in his palm, having every name he is going to vote for written on it. He has it down to the smallest electable slot: office to be filled, a dash or some dots, and a name. He does not need to know who the other candidates are or what the opposition thinks. Well in advance he has staked out his positions, listened to the sources he trusts, and he wants there to be no more fuss about it.

I don't know if he has ever missed a name. That would be a crisis. I would pay good money for the ballot to have a contest on it that he wasn't aware of. I would wait all day standing in the polling place, or propped in the corner, to see that. Like everything else, instead of stooping to indecision, he would sweep it away with anger, come up with a plan that for the rest of his uncomplicated life would make ironclad sense to him, ensuring this unfortunate, untidy circumstance would never happen again.

I gather he shows up even for primaries. How much idleness must a man be burdened with to show up to vote in a city council primary? With so few bothering to turn out, he has a disproportionate effect, and even those who tend to think the man is crazy lean into his cache of beliefs and wrangle around to see how they can collect a few here and a few there and maybe get this ever-voting, one-way fellow to toss the balance of the election their way.

His biggest worries appear to be a hardcore understanding of abortion, sex-education, and I think marriage equality, though he never speaks about the later. Whatever he gets riled about in any particular moment of conniption you can be sure is his mantra for the limited duration of that blessedly awkward conversation — or thundering unavoidable encounter. Only when he runs out of steam is there room for another issue to get whacked in the head with his profanity-driven orthodoxy shovel. But, most times, it is abortion that seems to lead the pack for him. The man is spit-chewing mad about that one. Takes up one whole room in his economy sized residential brain. It's a family matter, a bit of his past that still rubs raw, and he wants his revenge, I think.

Seems he has a daughter, and tried to raise the girl himself after his wife suddenly, and explosively, moved on. I hear the wife, finding good sense in second thoughts, left Stratem when the girl was about nine, taking off with Russell, the fellow who tried to set up a sheep farm one hill over. Russell never had much of a head for sheep, nor the business end of any transaction. But he looked in a pair of work jeans like a hundred dollars in a wallet made for fifty, and I think Mrs. Stratem could have been a bit full up by then with Stratem's surely straight-laced intentions. Russell and the still sturdy Linda Stratem were the talk of the town, though Stratem himself never heard much of it. When the bank took the sheep, Russell took Mrs. Stratem, and the last we saw was the old pick-up truck - that the bank was too late to repossess - hitting the main numbered road out of town: the two of them bobbing in Russell's fleeing Ford, like Russell's confiscated sheep unsteady in that strange, inelegant commercial stock-hauling rig the city branch of the bank had sent out with someone to fill with the sheep and Russell's truck - but sent them out too late for the truck.

The girl that they left with Stratem: even from that early age, she was never all that smooth to work with. You could tell she was a handful, and had ideas of her own. She had a way of looking back at you like she was searching for something in whatever you were saying, as though there were more to figure out than you were letting on. The meaning behind the simple seemed to have a draw for her. Behind her gray eyes were calculations.

Stratem, I suppose, did the best he could; but you could see the wildness in her. She got a library card without permission. She learned to deck herself out with make up, all on her own. She would go into the grocery store and stare at the magazine covers. Some nights she climbed out of the back window of her room and made off, footprints in the dew showing a track towards town. Now and again, she was gone the whole night. Stratem would come into town looking for her, carrying openly his birch switch. He would rummage about and knock on doors where he thought the local hellions lived. He would go rapping on car windows down by the cemetery and scared more than one couple into early ejaculation. During the day, teenagers would go up to his place to see for themselves that he was in fact a living local resident, and not some apparition come into town to keep them from getting a little lip lock on their latest puppy love partner.

Good people and bad talked about him and his switch. Most hoped he wouldn't find his daughter until the man's endless ire boiled down. But what do you do? He is a father, and he has a right. And he was as solid and unquestioning in his fathering as in his politics.

It was along about the time she was fourteen that she ran away for a whole week. That is a bit different from being out just for the night. Truth be told, I think most of those nights she was slipping away just to the barn to sleep in the loft, where she could wrap her thoughts like next week's blankets about herself, and feel where the warmth would be coming from. Maybe the barn was halfway between Stratem and town. The girl had her own sensibilities, her own geometry of mind; but it was wicked only to the extent that it was not Stratem's to mold. No one ever seemed to be afraid of the girl's well-worn thoughts, except the juggernaut that was Stratem.

But this was a whole week. Eight days and seven nights, put together in a string, and each one making Stratem madder than the one before. When she came back, a few fringe town residents said that they had looked closely over her in the weeks before she left, and said she had been showing just a bit of ill-timed fun pumped up under the lip of her midriff length shirt: but that she came back without that asymmetrical baggage. Personally, I never believed that she had the bump. I don't doubt she could have had something in the oven, but I would only know from the cock of the head, the sass in the hips, the mindfulness of the electricity around her, and not the bulge in her cast iron chassis. That would be too far along; but you know how people let their imaginations run loose, nosing over any garbage they can find, and often the prize petunias as well. I expect she just skipped for the second time in a row and decided to go to the clinic off route 17 about 60 miles up. I'd say she probably thumbed the whole way. Got picked up by a hopeful man here or there, letting his expectations carry her ten or twenty miles only to have those expectations unravel and go cold in the economy of her method. I'm sure she walked in as a charity case; and afterwards, while figuring what to do next, slept in alleys and backyards; and laid out two dozen futures for herself, like puzzles where only half the pieces came in the box – until, simple as rain, she realized no matter the final direction, she had to come one way or another home.

Though, more likely, one of the independent ladies here piled her in the family sedan; carried her to the young-girl-mistake-adjustment place; then let her hide in an unused back bedroom until both of them thought worry might get the better of outrage — and she would be safe in going back to Stratem's dark place. Or retreat there, with no other place for her to go, and options as thin as the sheep Russell once had tried to raise on bad feed, limited credit; or the ice fires Linda Stratem had for many likely dry, crowdedly lonely years, been holding back.

No one could lay a finger on any particular culprit, but with a girl that age you never know when they are going to get hormone happy, all chemically and emotionally wound up, and then fly apart, all on short notice. Could have been someone passing through. It might have been the unexpected magic of a blind date, or the high school Romeo on a bet. It is a small town, but we do have a football team. It wasn't me, and that's the best part of it.

By the age of sixteen, the girl was gone. Stratem was still using the switch, and I think his daughter had just outgrown it, and outgrown him as well. She was not a fragile thing, and I suspect it was properly time she cut ties with him. No one knows where she went. I hope she has a kind husband and a double-wide somewhere. I never thought badly of her.

But Stratem still talks at times of her. Not so much of missing the girl; or wondering where she went, or how she finally turned out; or of having had a daughter and lost her for reasons he hasn't enough gray matter to figure out; but instead monotonously listing all the efforts and methods he had devised and executed to keep her in her place: of how no one should be allowed to undo the lessons a father has to make plain; and how a man has to keep even his own daughter lashed to the line she must toe.

So now he just gets up early on election mornings, drives down to the polling station, and is usually the first one in line. Sometimes he is the only one in line. He parks his junk of a truck right in the front of whatever parking lot the polling station is tied to this time, and walks in, proud as a noontime rooster, past the poll workers: all of whom know better than to push a flyer his way, or ask if he knows how he is going to vote. He always has his crumpled piece of paper in his right hand, ready like an ivory-stock hand gun; and his mouth is set like a man with both a good breakfast down and the black sting of God's mission up.

The rest of us know that, if we haven't the time, or the weather is bad, or there is just too much else to do, Stratem will be the majority vote in town. Whatever conclusion he comes to, however he gets there, it will be our conclusion as well. The man stands proud as only the pot-bellied-certain can be; and when he moves, his thoughts roll about in his skull in units that clack together, making sounds like those of an old train hurtling towards new cargo. We think about that when we drive past him going purposefully into the polling place; and we promise ourselves to get up a little earlier next election, to get our day a tad more organized, and to actually come down to vote. We promise we won't be Stratem's peasants anymore. I think about his long-gone daughter, and the sly things she must have endured under his regal rule: the times she felt it best to crawl out of her window and head across the warming dark towards better times; and I admit that we all should consider the length and breadth of the issues, how our answers fall on our neighbors, and how we should take better care of one another. But we don't. We never do.

And what if, blocked or willing, the Stratem girl had stuck it out and had that rumored baby a few years back? Well, whether it looked a bit too much like Stratem himself or not, everyone figures he would have just gotten harder in his politics, and blamed the girl.

A THOUGHT PROCESS

She had a lot fewer problems when ideas were round. They were so much more comfortable. They rolled about in shared space with little impetus. They changed directions. They bumped into each other and all went in new, unpredictable arcs of the faintly possible.

Then came cubical ideas. Six sided thoughts and rectangular processes. These ideas tended to stay where you left them. They squatted. Colliding, their angular edges merely chipped; their surfaces wrinkled and quivered and the ideas simply shivered to a halt.

The old, reliable spheres might vary in size, but a sphere is a sphere. One spherical idea might be larger or smaller than another, but all of them obey the same simple geometry: they all act the same canonical way.

But these new box-like concepts were growing annoying. They lay about, in the way, shifting seldom, becoming roadblocks to safe conclusions. They leaned or they sat or they reluctantly slid, but never did they roll. They killed the fescue of the mind where they loitered.

She longed for the days when her best ideas touched down at only a point, bounded at the slightest push, and could spin through the full quiver of angles. She was comforted, in those days, by the great chaos of globes of thought jostling in lines all of unimaginable ordination, a great confusion of rollicking concepts busying about to no rest and no inevitable pattern.

And then one day she noticed two rectangular thoughts stacked one on top of the other, and she thought: oh no, these are building blocks.

CHICKENTOWN

There have always been rumors of Chickentown. If you were born around here, you grew up with the thought of it waiting just at the edge of the credible. Children are told that strange noises in the distance are free chickens, conferring. Any dog or cat that goes missing is credited as a loss to the insatiable hunger of our feral chickens. And a child too fond of misbehaving: well, malevolent chickens are known to lie in wait for children that no one would much miss.

After being an explanation for random occurrences; and then a source of fear that keeps children in bed under their covers at night, repenting every meanness they ever did; eventually Chickentown became a community legend. Half-jokingly, and a bit proud of the unique local tall tale, adults still recount the mythology to anyone who will sit still long enough to hear it, or will even tell the story again to themselves when they can't find an audience to corner.

The poultry farmers around here, in our distant, hard-currency past, kept chicken coops, and even had chickens loose in their back yards. The fowl listlessly busied about in the open space, came and went unsupervised at the coops. Feed was spread from an upturned apron. Of course, chickens were expected to lay, and a few that lagged in that endeavor ended up on the over-made after-church Sunday table; but for domestic chickens, the burden was bearable. Generations of chickens came and went without much distendable thought, as did a few dutiful generations of poultry farmers. It was a lazy, but comfortable history.

But every Paradise has a hitch in its stitching.

Taxes on the land kept going up, and the cost of outfitting children began to turn more and more on coin and less on homespun. Poultry farmers began to look at profit and loss as a concept well beyond the once comfortable mere sustainability of earlier years. The traditional ways made for a better man, but also a poorer man. Soon the coops were knocked down and replaced with huge barns egregiously filled with soulless ranks of wire cages. For our chickens, strutting aimlessly in the yard was replaced with waiting apprehensively at the wires. The apron, with its clouds of seed let fly like mists of goblin cheer, was replaced with a hose or a mechanical scoop, and the act of a chicken catching the meal was but a matter of pointing the bill always in the same brute direction.

Secretly, amongst themselves, the chickens would talk of the old ways. They would chatter nostalgically about the times they had known personally every rooster in the county, and every biddy in the yard; and compare those grander times to their new situation: with hundreds of ambiguous, un-introduced chickens stuck away in corners and rows and files and aware only of their immediate neighbors, chattering four-square gossip and unable to understand even the lengths to the darkly rumored far end of the warehouse.

The smart ones watched. The industrious ones plotted. The gifted ones studied their cages.

When a farmer would lose a chicken or two, it was not worth notice: at first. Loss of stock is a chargeable expense. It rolls off the balance sheet like spring ice in the river; it even makes husbandry seem more like a business of mechanics: statistical averages and clinical inputs versus bankable outputs. Every farmer simply loses a chicken now and again. This profession does not have to be an art inherited. Mistakes are made. Latches fail. A chicken gets away.

But soon the farmers noticed that the stock which would come up missing would be the strongest roosters, the boldest cocks, the best layers, the biddies with the most enduring broods. Breeding stock, prize winners, the egg producers that edged towards the high end of the production curve, the rooster siring the best poults: those chickens that turned easiest into profit, that settled on the desirable side of the production bell curve: those that gave back to the chicken-keeping enterprise the most hope.

But the bell curve was flattening for the poultry men.

On the lookout for cage breaks, after figuring something must be afoot, farmers would catch their chickens in the act, drag them back to dour reinforced prisons, or pull them aside for an unexpectedly rich Sunday dinner. It would be a time of feathers and cackling and an almost revengeful twisting of necks. Better to lose a good chicken to dinner than to lose that chicken to the wilderness. But some extraordinary chickens still got away. Some would make it to the woods. Some would be seen in a frenzy of free feathers disappearing with a flutter of faith into the dark of the brush line, their wings raised over the stubble at the edge of civilization, short hops of flight ejaculating them into the fringe of freedom.

No doubt many were slaughtered there. Foxes. Weasels. Poachers from other poultry farms. But the rumor always has been: some made it. And the ones that made it were the best, the brightest, the most determined, the strongest, the smartest, the luckiest, the ones that might mate like poultry-carrying freight trains. Their offspring would be mighty chickens, an admixture of all the traits that gave their parents this freedom, and those poults would rise to survive untended, feral and fierce and independent. And the best and most resourceful of those still in the factory farms and the farms' foul, brooding chicken huts, would yearn ever more brazenly to be free, spurred by rumors, rumors spread down through dispirited chicken-industry generations of spiteful chickens: a belief carried cage to cage as the spinal chance of the willing, the electric hope of the beaten, the enigmatic comfort of the exhausted. Chickentown. A break from the cage, a flit and a flight and a foundering from the warehouse, a race to the woods, a holy mad half-flying dash to the promised land. Eden. Nirvana. Imagination. Chickentown.

For townsfolk, Chickentown has been the darkening place too deep in the woods to be found: a place to take a well-primed first date, the source of unexplained wealth, the reason you are a day late and a dollar short. Surely, by now in everyone's imagination it is a chicken city of rare specimens: glorious predator chickens with nothing but pure, dominant chicken qualities bred arrow true for scores of generations. Chickens a poultry man cannot imagine, could not break, could not outsmart on his best chicken wrangling day. An independence, and perhaps even a mean streak, and a will to be peaceably feral. What centering example could we, as a community, have that might do any better to keep us uniformly crafted as one chilling, caring civility, than our own unwilling satellite — Chickentown?

Imagine our surprise when, as bold as bird leather, one day a lone chicken showed up, dragging behind him his lone cart, with the best and brightest eggs any of us – and some of us being four generations deep in chicken rearing - had ever seen. A chicken that stood upright and was willing to look the offspring of chicken tamers flat in the eye.

I and Joey and Nathan stood there, alone on the pitted road — halfway to nowhere, halfway back from nowhere — the chicken and we facing off like deacons on opposite sides of the church door on Sunday. We were the chosen ones to first meet this legendary chicken coming out as less than legendary; this figment of an entire countryside's playful imagination now corporeal and face to face with the town's most eligible and committed bachelors. We three of innocence and mischief. This one chicken that should not be outside of a fairy tale.

Those eggs were three times the size of factory-farm eggs, much deeper in color, better in geometry, and speckled with wholesome individuality. Eggs like that could not have come from any species of layer that we could understand using only our prime tools of a balance sheet and a bank loan. The master chicken stood there, coxcomb raised and his wings slightly parted, his tongue lifting barley out of the bowl of his open beak. We stared back, taking in the whole mythological length of this rogue chicken. At last, Joey bent slowly down and picked up one egg – no egg in particular — with thumb and forefinger, eyes set to collect that egg with just the right outwardly appreciative flourish, and yet watch the proud rooster at the same time; thumping the shell with the flat of his other hand's index finger, listening appreciatively to the returned sound in a way that only an egg-man can. We could hear the superiority of the product from three feet away. There was a timbre, as though the egg were proud to reflect the sound. He shook the wondrously heavy and pristine ovum, tapping it slightly against his forehead, listening to the wondrous thud, bringing it back to within inches of his best eye and slowly rolling it through his vision as though to wrap it in bedroom satin and thrust deliciously for home.

No better egg had ever come out of any fowl we might call chicken. It did not crack; it showed neither dullness nor illusory disquiet; and it seemed to quiver querulously, like a bride on the first workday morning of her stockyard marriage.

If all those years of rumor and fable and tales told to gullible children were true, it could work havoc on a collection of poultry men locked to a mortgage, a woman he married for farmland, a loan on his truck, and kids that spilled out too often and too unplanned. Chickentown as a real place? It could be the competition that runs the numbers staggering in on themselves and sets the banks to bloodlust. Those eggs could take our eggs in a fist fight, fair or not. When a once comfortable myth becomes a reality - and has a potential for real, balance sheet consequences - something has to be done, something has to be committed. A course of action is needed. A solution to what is not yet even a well-formed problem. Everyone has to think as quickly as a boy on a first date when he is confounded with the unexpected and casually menacing underwear hooks of his wonderfully half-drunk prize. This was no different, except it involved perhaps one hundred pounds of chicken.

Those of us gathered there in that first meeting of business and myth knew what had to be done. It may have come from a maturity beyond our years. It may have been the result of some feral survival instinct. It was as clear as a blind man seeing his wife through another man's climaxing eyes. Why, we would all be inheriting poultry farms one day. Soon enough, we would not be the sons of poultry farmers. We would be the poultry farmers.

So Joey delicately set the egg back into the viciously vacant space from which he had selected it. Suspiciously, he did not return to standing fully upright. He had twisted to let the power in his back seep into the trough of rotation. I could feel the charged, biomechanical wind as his hand whipped back to his old, hotly resented red clip knife, stuck always like a banner of advocacy half out of the tensely worn back public pocket of his blue denim jeans. Everyone envied that knife, and wished it were his. All the rest of us had were thin pocket knives, with no clip at all, and blades that weakened in the wind.

We knew everyone in town, and those in the rural combines, would eventually understand his vision, appreciate his quick understanding of the entire community's predicament. And we could make the best Sunday dinner ever, could fry up enough for half the county, using only this one poster-fowl of a chicken. Who would have to know about all these splendid eggs? No one, not here nor in Chickentown, need to be any the wiser. A week of egg-swaggering breakfasts, consumed on our rustic kitchen tables, set expecting the ordinary, and served the magical — and the marvelous evidence would be gone. Scrambled, fried, poached and boiled. And if anything more comes out of Chickentown, everyone needs to believe we will commit to giving them the same slash-across-the-gusset judgment. We do a good business here on our own, tapping out a tolerable existence with the motley industrial grade chickens we build our uncomplicated lives around. Any ungrateful birds that leave our sheltering nests need to stay gone.

We shared the rich blood from Joey's knife, splitting the corner off each of our shirts to each take a stain, folding the swatch carefully so the blood re-enforced itself and lay like a mark of startled courage pasted on the compact carrier. The eggs in their cart, the chicken bled out on top, and the magical stain in our pockets. Nothing more is ever needed for all to be right with the world.

On nights when the dark is alcohol damp; and a fresh date's line-of-sight is fractured by privately noisy and uneasy woods; and when any snap and grumble in the brush seems pointed specifically at a cooing couple; with the car's front seat stinking of stretching out like a feather bed; and all the dread of childhood Chickentown terrors feeling less like interruption and more like the mounting integers of opportunity: why, on many nights like that, this closely couraged stain has more than once gotten me lust-burrowing past third, and lizardly home.

LEARNING

We were once the land of not knowing. Long years ago our ancestors were visited by the first out-world explorers and did not know the man and his horse were not one thing. Then, when the man dismounted, our forefathers did not know why the horse would willingly bear the man's weight. It was to them a science of conclusions, with no equation leading to the sum. How such things inserted themselves into our ancestors' regular world, our ancestors did not know.

Our histories tell us that centuries passed, thick with novelties. Religion came, and we did not know God could be kept in a book, or that He lived in a specific house. Sailors and merchants came and we did not know of the boils and buboes we would suffer through our commerce with them, nor of the sailors' and merchants' right to appropriate our wives and daughters and fledgling boys. Nor did the people know why, over time, even the People –once dark and muddy and proud — prized blue eyes, fragile skin, and a specter of sun running triumphantly in the hair.

Medicines came and we did not know why they could turn an ordinary passing into a miracle resurrection. Then new crops came and we did not know that we would have to trade them at a premium to an out-world intermediary for the crops we grew before in our backyards. We did not know commerce was a way of some getting more, most getting less.

And when our lands became company lands, we did not know the laws that made them become so. When the plantation keepers set up a voice box so we could know the world better, all we knew was the sound of the world we did not get to know. Some of our children - as full of the out-world words and disengendering rhythms as an uncracked wife with her quivering first husband - went out to find the out-world, and we did not know we would never hear of them again. Some of our women-girls disappeared into the plantation houses and we did not know we would see them only again as ghosts on the plantation porches, or worming their way to or from a distant market with unknown bags which they carried as if each girl was an inedible pack animal.

But we are now a knowing village. Each of us has our claim on some knowledge. Collectively, we have our lore. On a small part of what was once our land, we are left — only the old, retired now from not knowing, little more than un-evicted: alive with the certain, happy with what grand conclusions we know and have become. It has taken generations to learn so much.

Come see us. We have history. There is a brochure.

THE SPECIMEN HUNTER

In retrospect, Lost Hope station was a raucous galleon of light; a hyper charged wire of activity; a mass of gleeful emotions and unbounded celebration; and a star burst of mathematically noble debauchery.

Its two-slot docking bay, with the occasional unpredictable ten percent variance in artificial gravity, was an architectural novelty that usually loomed vacant; but which seemed, when it was needed, to be needed always by one too many; and so everyone waited in the docking lottery. The leveling supports moved as slowly as a drunken Therosian cephalopod, and with about as much coordination, strut to strut. If what you were landing weren't junk, you would never trust it to the junk you were landing it on.

But six months out into deep space, with the black of the Universe outside as thick as a mohair blanket and the quiet as deep as the screams of potbellied clams, the whole docking deck suddenly seems like a rival to the Pristine Spires, an artistry of Corvan Supermen, a paean to Gaudi on speed. I would give my return-trip pay to have those solid straps around my ship, to feel the artificial gravity grab, as off key as it might be, the flat of my bowels and settle the swirl of my brain with a seriously intended true up and true down.

Even worse, it now seems every man and every woman on Lost Hope must have been a high school quarterback, or the defiantly flaxen haired captain of the cheerleading team. Each broken down hag, left having to work the comfort stations at the very rim of the Universe, now is remembered as having legs that went on forever, non-synthetic chests, real teeth with stylish pseudo fangs, and so much energy it seemed as though they were internally fired by rogue isotopes. Their personalities stank of good cheer. Whatever a customer paid was a bargain; though, at the time, you might be thinking that only scarcity and distance could make out of this rot any value, and that these reeking vendors should be glad there is a dead end of the Universe to make their wares have some reluctant, terribly relative, worth.

Six months into a trip no one has taken before, to no place no one knows, for no reason other than to find out if there is a reason to come out here at all: a place like Lost Hope becomes a vacation spot, a happily remembered way-station of mottled aromas and pleasant personalities, happily supplied with people who sometimes kill each other and always over charge and then send a happy traveler on his or her exciting way, if there is no incentive not to do so.

Understand: this is part of my frame of reference. In six months I have learned the sound of every warning alert on this ship, have counted the heartbeats between operating cycles, can predict what arm of the dust is soon to resettle itself. I have gotten over the glorious vision of myself as the intrepid explorer, the heroic vanguard of my species, the thick-chested representative of all that is right with humanity. I am cockroach rubbery from the tasteless food I have eaten. I am hard on all my edges from the air baths I take to keep free what little water I carry. I thrive on 'adequate' alone. It makes me what I am, and I have lost the glittery illusions of my being anything else. In this comparatively sterile environment, I am more the animal that I secretly am deep within myself than I would be anywhere else I might choose to lie in wait.

And then there is you. On this gray little world, I have seen, logged, and discarded a dozen uninteresting life forms. I have watched your native ether eaters wave in their shallow seas. I've seen your skimmers bounding in the amalgamated atmosphere as though they might be happy, though I am in no state for happy. I have cruised through schools of lackluster worm needles that did not have the self-appreciation to scurry out of my way as my ship carved its thunderous ruts fatally through them. There is nothing here, it would seem, soullessly lurking about that a privateer, or a mineral hound, or a commercial exo-biologist, or even a circus barker, could use. And then I found you.

You are the first thing I have seen since Lost Hope with two legs, with verticality, with a head on what seems to be a quartet of shoulders. The ridges that ride teasingly over your eyes are not unlike eyebrows. The smooth of your blue skin seems to shimmer with tactile possibilities: tight across a body that, in the dark, might feel more human than my own overly familiar and voyage-worn outline. Even the feathering of your four tentacles, independently restless at your waist, is not unseductive: and I can at times be mesmerized with watching them whip sensuously adrift in their intertwined tethering patterns.

I know that in the movement of those delirious tentacles there is some language, that there is some way for us to speak. There is an old saying on the far-out space docks that similar needs breed similar designs. I have seen it. The entire Universe goes about its work in much the same fashion no matter what particular splash of stars is at the moment overhead. It works its common will perhaps with a different color or a different texture, with an extra covering or a different number of digits. But a good design persists. Corner to corner, the Universe promotes the same unconscious ends.

You stand knee deep in as much of your planet's native fluid as I could rake into the containment vessel. What was your sea outside is now our lake inside. It will have to be drained before stasis is applied for the long, pleasureless trip back to Lost Hope. But, for a short while, we can see if we can delicately decipher each the other, find common purpose and ends, can make passable companions: the specimen and the captor. There is an old earth saying: if you were the only girl in the world, and I were the only guy, well, maybe......

This ship is our world now. A world I know too well. I stink of the moans and shrieks of metal with purpose but no feeling, with utility but no comfort, with days of mathematically pure intentions piled dry and unlikable in the hold. And I think I can translate the pattern of that intrigue-prone bioluminescence shivering at the edge of your forehead; like a man making small talk in a bar, I can painstakingly contrast it for meaning against the agitation in your school-girl lithe tentacles. Your elegantly deep eyes, through the containment glass, flick about the magisterial whole of me; and I think they see in my feral designs and purposes something familiar, something with ends and means that you, in some dark galactic arm's rhythm, have a spark of warm sisterhood with. Even though contained in this alien world with me - the alien - and shielded with only a piece of your planet, you have within you still your time-spanning senses and needs, your relentless yearnings for self-replication, the pounding spin of your purposely greedy biology. As do I.

Well, maybe.

THE RESCUE

There is no way to go on loving in a burning building, but we do. We worry more that the sheets are unjustly knotted, than that there is smoke crawling like omnivorous, dream-stealing spiders across the ceiling. We worry that the blankets will never be used again; that our memories, woven into them like the smell of a corpse littering the trunk of a car, will go out of existence with the ashen cloth. We worry we are forgetting sheets blankets and memories even now, and being ourselves forgotten. We are twisted through the variations executed in the mere simplicity of our present accomplishment, and, buried within our perception of even the burning building, our paper hero antics are lost inside the needful anatomy fulfilled by thousands of lackluster generations acting out in the panoramic tunnel vision of individual needs. We are of no need, but all of you need our act of un-selfed selfishness.

When you, my brave fireman, look in from the municipal fire truck ladder, the glass window already vibrating from heat, you will not think of saving us. You will understand the flames and our frenetic cross-stitchery and think: how intricate. Or, you will think how beautiful the disharmonies of people meeting a simple animal imperative can be. Or, you will think omigod, the place is on fire and how murderously they hump. Or, you will think again this is a line and not points on a line. Or, you will think nothing at all.

Then, from the microphone tethered to your shoulder like a favored flagellum, dispatch will tell you: there is no way to go on loving in a burning building.

WHY DO YOU DO IT?

"Why do you do it?" I ask of the man's backside as he stands on the bumper of the truck and reaches way in to find a prime leg and snake it over all of the other parts in the truck bed. When he finally has it firmly in two hands, he half-twists back towards the parking lot behind him and tosses the appendage in an exaggerated arc – so that, when it lands, it hardly slides, but simply rattles a bit on the pavement.

These are not heavy items. Alloys intended to be light. He simply has so many of them.

"Where have you been collecting them today?", I ask. He smiles, like he does not know the language. It is a game. I will have to guess. And, when – finally - I am close enough to knowing where he has collected all of his prizes, the gates will open up and his description of the back doors and holding bins and reserve sheds will sound like a man describing the steak he lingered passionately over the night before, or the blinding memory maps of the once unknown surface tension of a serendipitously, suddenly acquired lover.

He slides over to the side of the truck bed and one-hands a shorter piece, reverse sway pitches it easily out onto the mostly empty lot.

"You would not stand so close if you knew where I had been hunting today." He is joking as much as he can joke, but I back up a few clipped steps anyway.

He has the last piece he seems to want and jumps down from the truck. With mock confusion, he looks over each subunit of machinery from a distance and finally reaches into his pocket for the master boot controller. I watch him and his economic moves more than I watch the pieces of machinery. The man seems to love his scrap so.

Once he lights the electric to the collection with his controller, he crouches, and then casually puts the animation device back in his pocket. He leans forward, his hat turned backwards, his hands on his knees, his eyes moving about like fish in an aquarium set within the confines of his perfectly still face. His smile seems painted thickly in unerupted passion.

"Let's see what they make now, let's see what they make." He moves enough just to quickly clap his hands, then places them back on his knees.

On the pavement, one section of incomplete machinery seems to have decided it is, in fact, a leg; and another piece may not be sure what it is, but seems to have identified another, slower companion piece as a backbone. The appendages scan each other, looking for connection points. They negotiate wirelessly who should be where, what is the best collective configuration. There are milliseconds of argument, nanoseconds of confirming protocols. Harmonies evolve.

"You know," he hollers across the slowly moving abandoned artifacts at me, "I have no idea why they so fiercely want to be together."

Two legs have developed and left now is what could be one long arm and one short arm. They may have earlier too soon opted for which piece was to be the backbone. At this point it cannot be helped. The longer arm connects itself to the backbone with its own sealing screws and the shorter arm is not far behind.

When it finally stands, the scrap man happily says 'Well, welcome to the vertical, my big brother. Let's see what we can use you for." I wait for an answer, but it would be too much to find a speech processor on one of these pieces. Those usually go with the cranial console - the head - and heads are usually cleaned out before they are set loose for the scrappers.

"The food processing plant?" Surely from the suggestion of the magnificent scrap collector, I think I see a scoop on one arm.

"No."

"The pavement mixer?"

"Jimmy, Jimmy, Jimmy. Would a pavement mixer be this clean?" He is only half mocking me.

"Guess." He tilts his head sideways to look at me out of only one eye.

"The petrochemical auxiliary on Thurston Street."

"And you think they would let me in there with a scrapper's truck and license?"

"Well, it really does not matter where they come from, because they reconfigure when you alter their parts." I know this. He knows this. Everyone knows this. But he has some odd fascination with origins.

"Guess."

The two long appendages that are now legs might be a clue. Two blocks over is Drury and Drury, a brick manufacturer, making antique looking bricks out of a collection of polymers, laced with nano-carbon, supporting spines of invisible organic adhesive. They run through robots like a crematorium goes through nanites.

"Drury and Drury."

He angles his head higher and raises a finger to point at me. "Now, boy, you are thinking. Three weeks ago, it would have taken you two more guesses. It was the long appendages, eh?"

I look about to see if it could have been anything else. Rational thought is a deceptive thing. Where any idea comes from is always suspect, and what I think may have led me to a good guess might be something other than what my mind tells me it was. Minds lie. "Yes, that was it. I knew what they were for." After I had gazed at them for a while, their potential use had come to me like an intercepted drunken thought.

He reaches into his pocket and shuts down the self-assembled robot with a click on the console still safely stifled in his pants. No need for theatrics now. The ritual was over. Now is the decision.

"Well, I saw one more piece I'd like to add to this one, and I may have to swap in something for that short arm, but I think I like this one. And you recognized him as Drury." He winks at me, and he only winks when he is exceptionally pleased.

"I think I might find a head for our former brick assembler. One of those one-lens, deep set types, with auxiliary connection ports set out like ears. Maybe with some extra memory and a bigger processor, so it does not have to argue with its subsystems for shared computing cycles."

He steps a bit back and regards the length of the collection, still running mentally through design possibilities. He has collected the pieces, selected the pieces, let the pieces organize themselves, and now he was in charge again, in full control of the finalization. "You know, you came from Drury. You could have a brother here."

Or a sister. Even a final, finished unit - assembled of all the lost original pieces reconnecting and coming up with a single coordinated purpose – like myself still wants to fit in ever more perfectly. It does not make any difference to me: brother, sister. Or a friend, two manufacturing series out of synchronization. But to be one of two and not simply one of one — now that is a thing to prize. I tap my long metal fingers against the brush of my recognition. A bit always dark takes fire. I begin disastrously to hope the man may need another like me around the shop.

PREPARATIONS OF A TERRORIST

She stands by the window, the sweat rolling down her dark, naked back, her hands driving beads of it out of her skin along her threadbare hips through the simple contact embraced in a woman's unthinking posture. And it is not the sweat of our industrial sex, now interrupted, yet incomplete and still tangled in imagination. It is the sweat of one window only available to open, no breeze, the city's empty streets radiating back the done day's heat, the air grimy with an atomization of raw oil.

She settles into this environment, becoming a piece of it, a piece of it consuming itself. She is a numbers game. I see her like a clock face. The heat considers her simply someplace new to be.

I have seen air conditioning. When I was appointed a company leader in the army of Anyplace, I was called for instructions to the division seat of authority. I was led into a small room that held our regional leader, his brightly outlined lieutenants, and an air conditioning unit. The unit hummed and shivered and occasionally spat, and water pooled beneath it. I could barely concentrate on the instructions I was being given, consumed with marveling at the cold. As I later thought more about it, the cold was probably uncomfortable – but it was impressive, and it stood as a symbol of all that could come with the ascendancy of Anyplace. I remember the hair littering my arms stepping out to luxuriate the length of itself in the brief miracle. The air itself tickled. It was the lick of a dog after feeding.

If this wanton technology could be brought here, where the dust has tenure and the heat is happy in every fold of every grandmother's skin, then Anyplace can accomplish anything.

The girl turns again towards me and I can see that her nakedness is uneven, her sex is unbalanced, her lines are unsteady and at times indistinct. Her shadow would not fold well. She must have passed me her name earlier, must have whispered it at me like a scold set loose on phantom ice. I try to remember it. I try. How many syllables? How many letters? The taste of her skin is anthracite, and brings no memories.

She does not mock me, nor does she imagine me incapable. She is calculating: time invested, time yet to be invested, the course of the heat, what is to happen after the stilled vibrations of our commerce. What is to happen after. The night stretches out like a ladder. She hopes that the room will remain hers. She plans to resettle the sheets, pull the mattress away from the wall. She plans of perhaps yet more commerce, and laughs silently at the plans of yet more commerce. I am the bridge between two other moments, the measurable moments on either side of me and my unraveled meaning. For her, I have no lasting meaning. She has no thought of me at all. Or, if she does have thought, it is not mockery, not malice, not complaints of inexperience. It is time spent, options missed, calories invested. I am a comma in her day's existence, a mark that makes a string of words roll off the tongue with mildly enhanced clarity.

The lifeless do not mock the living.

My rise and fall, the rise and fall of any part of me, is without compare. To compare does her no good. I wonder how this might go if she were a better woman. She does not know what a better woman is, nor how you make one from the scraps she has at hand. And so our worlds pass.

She paired with me holding only the hope of getting paid. The city is beyond established prices, beyond establishing price. The pay for any commercial good is charity. The army of Anyplace has moved through the city, driving filth before it, and is now four miles away in the city's satellites. Only those of us with orders to the rear are left to be customers. Empty streets shackle empty streets, and only the vendors of contraband and those who prey upon those delirious, forsaken citizens who come out to shake their desperation clean of other men's dirt, are out and about and at work quietly in the leftover light.

My advantage is that she must take a chance. In the dirty brilliance of a dingy evening, she looks like something captured, something trapped in this room. Unthreatened and with a reserve of strength, but trapped nonetheless. Without moving, she paces. Without clear thought, she plots. I motion her back to the bed and I can see staggering across her indistinct skin merciful quivers of hesitation. I think she already understands that, after loving like a dog, I will dress like a soldier, and march solemnly out, leaving none of the money even now I do not have.

She is my permitted indulgence, the night of grace before the fullness of mission. Usually, it is not allowed to appease one's flesh, unless it is done in the service of Anyplace. Our urges and un-blunted needs are not to be wasted, are not repulsive when applied in the service of Anyplace. One tenant of leadership is to understand that service to Anyplace in itself provides all absolution.

I am in service to Anyplace, and I am due her. I am a leader. I am at the rear to prepare for my morning's mission. I have found and trained many recruits for Anyplace. I have killed more enemies of Anyplace than I can remember. I will be tomorrow an example to all who either know or do not know the wonders of Anyplace. I will be like that burst of air conditioning that so captured my arms and hair and was uncomfortably comforting. I am preparing myself. I prepare myself. I prepare.

I am full with my coming mission and my member rises to new attention. It stands there, saluting what I have yet to do. The girl believes its sudden re-invigoration is her doing. Let her believe. She brings one hand to her mouth and pushes out in universal seduction the hip she still holds. She begins to drift back around the bed, brushing her thigh along the uncovered mattress, an animal rush of overused air emitting luminously from her mouth.

This time I will finish. I know I will sustain myself to the end. I must. I will work a fever through both of us, the two of us united hands and arms and feet and mouths: a blur of myself and mission and the success of Anyplace. I will burst my rage into her. I will empty out a part of me and make room for more of Anyplace to flood back within. At that sharp moment, my explosion will be my mission, the genetic completion of my duty to Anyplace. We will howl together at the triumph of everyone.

I will feel the mission that is to be, hard as our oceans, beginning to cloud and merge with the mission that has been, and the wild breath of me will, at my will, return to an order and calm. I imagine her lying on her back, breath already stilled from the practice of being unaffected, untouched in the touching. I can smell the simplicity of her sweat, the mechanics of the tedium her body across ever widening histories manages to be, though she expends no effort and no will to fall into such an abyss of use and uselessness. And then I will rise and return to my clothes, dressing like a school boy reciting his mathematics. She will lengthen on one arm, watching, trying to look impressed though she is not impressed, not by any part of this but the earning or lack of earning, and we both will breathe without heroism the stench of our shared but unequal disappointments.

And when I leave, neither of us will be better or worse, diminished or enlightened. And all that anyone will know of it is that, soon, I will have a mission: she is a part of the land that makes room for it. I have wedded her in her ignorance to my work, wedded her as the splendidly durable wife a man of my many missions' merits.

THE MEASURE

He had been curious about the Society of the Left Hand for as long as he could responsibly remember. Born ambidextrous, he wondered if his experiences were all that segregated from those of the truly left handed, from those with a weakened right appendage, and what in their collective commonalities would drive them to fathom and maintain their own identification society. His hands dangled equally beside him, and that, perhaps, is all the difference in the world; or, perhaps, it is nothing.

He had nearly turned back at the stoically massive entrance: its hinges on the right and its lock laboring on the left. When he had pressed the severely lavished visitor announcement button, he recoiled like cold from hot iron as the two tone herald rang the lower note first and the higher note second, reversing the pander of all the summoning heralds he had heard from all the houses he had ever visited: houses with owners of either handedness. The noise baffled him like the bittersweet howls of prisoner angels. He stood, shifting balance equally between his feet, ready to call the affair off, to wrap his curiosity back into the flap of his handkerchief and stuff it again into his pocket: to wait until he were safely down the road to take it out and inspect it again, when the liberty to physically experience it had securely passed and there would be no cost to his unmeasured puzzlement.

He had begun to think that 'left' was not a matter of merely the favored hand. The concept of 'left' had been turned around, spirited over the left shoulder of some meticulously scheming brute, and made into a way of life: something the great mass of the left handed would never take to heart; but which, among the believers, plodded stealthily along, ostensibly in the unknowing left handeds' good names. There would be secrets to keep; scores to settle; a howling, incendiary narrative that demanded a join of forces. Those of the left way of life would manufacture their shadows differently than did others; their house pets would counter-rotate.

As he fondled his options, the door opened.

The dark stood un-menacing. At the far end of the revealed hall, he could see a lighted rendition of God passing life to Adam: he recognized the copy. This painting was on the wall, not a ceiling, and it spread out like its mission were the wall, and the wall suckled it. Yet, in this rendition, God lazily reached out with His extended left hand. The painting was as dull as the sex of water clinging to the underside of basalt: but it was unmistakable, reverent, matter of fact, and come-hither all at the same time. It insisted. It told its story like a left-handed stripper at a peep show. It instructed. He was its subject and he drew in the spectacle as if it were perfume on the tongue.

He started to twist away, back to the busy city street and its lack of mysteries, but already from deep within the richly intermittent dark someone with the voice of tinfoil was demanding, slowly and beyond challenge, that he hold out both hands: that he let the assembled gray voices of the Society review each set of digits to see which hand revealed the most wear. His toes curled under him. What could he do? He had those hands - neither of them favored nor ill-favored, neither of them friend nor a birthright enemy - safely at his side. But he unthinkingly raised his suddenly blood drained extremities together, extending them away from his growing, unruly confusion; and into the unbendable cause of the magnificent entryway. He spread his fingers and he felt, not unkindly, the light at his back, the dark at his face. And he waited. The weight of the horror of his inexcusable balance collecting on his back like the sons of single-handed scarecrows, he waited.

THE GIFT OF A COW

"Mr. Tingler, please wake up."

Mary was standing in the open doorway, her two hundred or so pounds centered in the huge opening. The morning sun leaked in from behind her, curling around her roughly cylindrical body as though to grasp her and pull her back out of its way. Or maybe pull her back from the withered threshold and mercifully shut the door.

"Mr. Tingler, you need to wake up. It is good in the morning already."

I was watching her through the slit of one eye. She would not know that I was watching her, but she would think it just possible. Beside me on the left, what's-her-name was awake but not moving: I suspect so not as to disturb me. On the right, what's-her-name was twisted away from me on her side, but her head was turned back enough that I could see the mouth was open, and air was rushing in and out in only the way it can without conscription in a sleeping person.

"Mr. Tingler. Mr. Tingler. It is Mr. George again. Mr. George has lost track of his cow. Mr. George worries the dogs will get his cow. Mr. George worries himself into twitches about that cow, Mr. Tingler."

Mary had not moved since establishing her blocking position in the door way. I would bet the better of my two bed guests that the door had already been partially open when she arrived and that she had pushed it the rest of the way without actually stepping in. She would not be surprised that I was in bed, merely four spectacularly easy yards from the door, with two women. Mary has seen this before. She has caught me committing sex acts with her neighbors' wives on the ceiling. She has disinterestedly watched as I would try to land, from a thousand feet up, without breaking anything or anyone while just at the point of enthusiastically passing a wealth of my genetic material to the town scold. Nothing can surprise Mary.

They call me Mr. Tingler for the previously unknown sensation I leave in women at the extinguishing end of sex. With my super human strength, I long ago learned to control my ferocity of passion in the act; to understand my own super human spine, and hips, and barrel gripping hands, and pyrotechnically dazzling speed; and to hold back the ballistic force of my stream. Gut one or two love partners and you start looking for the cause, considering the alternatives, rethinking just how you might go about this when paired with a normal person. I can never be fully mindless, driven purely by the hyperbolic. In my most frenzied, I have to be calm, to calculate, to project likely outcomes and imagine nearly architectural tolerances. I have to be most careful when I am engaging in something enthrallingly acrobatic, such as fevered coitus-in-flight, or mounting my moment's mate from a hovering start. Of course, no woman can say she isn't somehow thrilled to have a lover start his entry from two miles away and make a hole-in-one with a single vital, smooth arrest. But if I am off by just half an inch: oh my.

Is it for the women I am here, you ask? Why, no. In the big city women are even easier: there are more of them, and they have more wickedly fragile minds. They have so many more reasons for wanting to be a hole in the mattress, a well-worn sheath, a place to dump excess gladdening fluid production. No: the women out here farm and herd and struggle and think sex with me is a part of life, not the end of it. I may be super human, but in the end I am providing as much of a service as they are. I am a natural phenomenon. They work with me, or around me, or sometimes past me. It makes physical sense to them.

So why then be out here, with all my super powers, in a dirt village thirty miles in any direction from the nearest electricity and running water, living with a bunch of half-naked savages, even if they might appreciate me for what I am far better than would a society with newspapers and make up and stiletto heels and coffee shops, you ask?

Have you ever been to a suburban Discount Emporium on a Saturday night?

Snap that picture and bring it back here to compare. Give these people a hoe, and they will plant beans. Give the Emporium browsers democracy, and they will create a plutocracy: all while wearing spandex and bedroom slippers in public.

No, let me be a super hero where everyone has just the smarts they need, where the talent matches the audience. I get to do simple things, and be loved. Why don't you go solve the political downside of investment inflation in an economy predicated on privatizing gain and socializing loss, with risk mitigation rising to be one of the financial sector's most highly securitized activities? See who loves you.

So here stands Mary, with a mission about Mr. George. I roll over on my side and grab what's-her-name on the right by her considerable nearest breast, softly rolling the smooth of it into a dimple and pinching across the fold I have made at her flat, joyfully pouting nipple, and whisper in her ear, "Don't go. Or, if you go, be back tonight." I say nothing to what's-her-name on the left. Not that there is anything wrong with her. But if you want one to feel special, you have to make one feel un-special. Don't worry. Later in the week I'll pop up onto what's-her-name-on-the-left's freshly thatched roof, coo into her back window, and ask her to come out, come out, come out for a whirlwind writhing at the river bank, followed by a show of how I make mini-waterspouts in a calm, unsurprised wash-water stream.

"Mr. Tingler?"

So I sit up and say, "Morning, Mary. Is something amiss?" I appear, as always, instantly awake, instantly attentive. Truth, justice, honor, service, all those things.

"Mr. George: he says his cow is in danger. I don't know. Mr. George has a lot of trouble with that cow."

Yes, he does. If Mr. George lived in a modernized country, his cow by now would be on an old age pension. Mr. George's cow was an experiment in cow longevity long before I showed up. Skin and sticks, the balsawood cow would be too little to slaughter. But, around here, your cow is your sign of wealth, and we can't let Mr. George think he is as poor as he obviously is. And I think Mr. George is simply used to the cow's company.

I've built Mr. George a fence, but he likes to let his cow roam outside the fence. I guess it gives Mr. George a belief in, perhaps, the cow having a sense of freedom. It is a cow. It wants fodder, water, a place out of the rain, the death of flies, and an ability to sleep much longer than other cows. A sense of freedom I don't think comes in its cast of features, or in its list of wants. It ambles, it doesn't wander.

Mr. George needs to take care of that cow. He needs to use the fence I have built him, and latch the gate, and then he can spend all evening whispering sweet nothings into the cow's ear. I have told him I can't fix everything. I can shore up a house. I can unblock a river. I can empty a latrine. I can find wood from the receding forests miles away. I can resolve territorial disputes – maybe not fairly, but resolve them nonetheless. But I can't fix everything. I am a super hero. Not a mind reader. Not a doctor. Not a faith healer.

Every time I bring the sad, old cow back, Mr. George thanks me, and his granddaughters come running over to have a romp in the bed. Not that I am taking advantage of them. This is a simple society: the best specimens breed, the least are left to have sex with themselves. There is no subtlety here, no hidden agendas that, in reality, no matter where they are played out would all default to exactly the same mantra as the one they live by in this village. In the big world, there are forty-seven steps to what here is a two-step process. It all ends the same place.

So I climb out of bed. Mary does not look away. She has seen all of me before. I rummage around for my tights, while a thin wisp of a man we call Hollow Jim joins Mary, blocking out a little more of the light. He stands there in a loincloth, with a walking stick, waiting to see if I need anything. All the men around here at one time wore codpieces, and his used to be so long it jutted into the room like an antenna. Ever since I established a routine and started working my way through the village's eligible women, and a few not so eligible, the codpieces went away. Some were real works of art, so heavy that, if a man did not rig the support right, he could be pissing around corners for weeks. I know they mean nothing so long as I am around, but I miss them. I liked the thought that someone would go through all that trouble. If I ever leave, perhaps the fashion will come back into vogue.

The walking sticks now are the rage. I have not figured those out quite yet.

"So, Mary, where did Mr. George say he last saw the cow?"

"Mr. George, he didn't say. Mr. George says the cow was inside the fence last night, and this morning there is no cow."

Mr. George probably left the gate open. He gets distracted. It would serve him right if the stray dogs got the cow. I have my cape on just a bit catawampus, but the aerodynamics of flight will straighten it out. I smooth my tunic and pull my sash around the right way. One what's-her-name is resting on an elbow, and the other has curled half into a ball and is sleeping like it is the last thing that was asked of her. I've gotten a bit twisted, and have to think about which is what's-her-name left and which is what's-her-name right. It's a round room. Anyone can get disoriented if you forget about the door.

"Well, Mary, tell Mr. George that I will do my best. But remind him of what I've been telling him: one day that cow is going to be gone. I can do a lot of things, but some things I cannot do."

"Alright, Mr. Tingler. I tell him. I tell him, too, that you be straight back." Her faith is like that of someone with absolutely nothing beyond this kernel of faith to have faith in.

Mary stands aside as I edge towards the door. Hollow Jim backs up, then backs to the left. He came by I am sure just to see the take-off. These people never seem to tire of it.

I step two steps out and then I'm off, faster than a scalded dog out of a blind man's kitchen. In the air, I can feel my body stretch out, the vertebrae lengthen, my ankles and feet shake themselves free of gravity. I let my cheeks vibrate in the howling wind that my speed makes. Last night, and even today, and whole stretches of my plaid past, fall away and I am an element of nature at this moment, as natural as the sun, as natural a force as gravity or magnetism or rainbows. I feel the molecules of the air.

It would serve Mr. George right if I found that cow half eaten a mile down the road. Or better, if I found the cow walking in circles at forest edge, wondering what to do, and I gathered him in my arms and flew him thirty miles to some other village, dropped down into some other hovel's empty paddock, and said, "Here, take this gift of a cow.

Prosper from it." The villagers would eye me with wonder and wonder why I would bring such a useless and nearly dead cow to them. How much more happiness would there then be, and I would not have to worry about that insatiably long-lived cow again. But that's not me. I am a super hero after all. Hero is the important word here.

I focus. I am looking for fearfully small signs of cow track. I am two hundred flipping yards in the air, and I can focus for tiny tracks in dry dust. I see so much that I marvel at the amount of activity there is in this place of no activity. See, tracks from an old, idled crow. A beetle, dragging a leaf, unstartled by anything or anyone, in its world the size of a man's chest. And the smell of two rats, thinking to hitch a ride in a fat man's cart. There, a speck of dung from a cow. And wrapped accidentally around it, the scent of a woman bathing. I foil the air and come about, better than any man's missile could on the scattered molecules of cow leavings. Sometimes I amaze even myself.

Soon, I will make everything revealed. Revealed. And I am thinking on the back channel, cod pieces to walking sticks and a super hero at the middle of it. I do get myself into some straits that super human strength just cannot get the better of. Nor would I want it to.

WORD CRIME

He hated to be here. The stalls were uneven, some narrow, some wide, some with a draw curtain, many with a rope stretched side to side with hanging rags on that rope as a door front. Many looked like they would come down if a sneeze fell against them.

At some, vendors peered out, looking sheepishly side to side, ready to give the alarm if the police came wandering through. Others sat back in the chattering dark of their stalls, prepared to consider the breadth and width and smell and need of an exploring potential customer – each professionally certain they would recognize the repeat customer, the thrill buyer, the undercover agent.

The silence was expectantly oppressive, as it always is in these knock-about markets. This was not a place where words were wasted; but neither were they pristinely cherished. You could find warily dissimilar verbs sold together in the same overwrought matchbox. Prepositions lay barely a decibel deep in thimbles. Nouns of mismatched species could be found forced together in the same tattered envelope. As little respect for the words as for the customers.

Every time he had to come here, he promised himself he would forever more marshal his words more wisely. But at least every other month he would come to some dry midweek with his seven-day quota of words spent. He could certainly remain unspeaking until his quota was restored for the next week. But he loved telling his neighbors' children to get off his precious lawn, or making amorous suggestions to his wife, or politicizing at work. Oh, he could make gestures and broadly act out desired outcomes. But words were immediate: they slithered into the outline of a process, they bounded about as meticulous orders.

So here he was, buying jumbled black-market words – words that ruefully taciturn people had left over from their quotas, words orphaned by sudden death, words taken by force from those unable to protect them.

If only the Government or some reputable corporate entity managed the reclaimed unused words – but it was illegal to reclaim words. They could only go to surplus storage, be resorted, be placed into the common warehouses, be resupplied to the public in individual quotas. But there were back channels.

He passed the first few stalls without looking. The early stalls are the most picked over, favorites with the grab anything and get out crowd, the scared, the first-timers. He selected a stall about a third of the way into the line of illicit shops. It had a full, not overly threadbare, curtain to restrain its private inner chambers from the street proper. It looked like its owner had customized much of its rickety skeleton for quick set-up and take-down. Perhaps its owner had a plan to take his inventory and stall quickly to freedom if the police appeared and began working the end of the line. Down and packed and off into the dark between legitimate businesses.

Plastic cups of verbs, coffee cans of nouns, a petri dish of adjectives, an old pill bottle of adverbs.

Of course, no one could be sure of potency, or even gender, or consistency. An adverbial gets mixed in with a verb. A preposition is tangled with a noun. An amen corner of pronouns falls in with a gang of adjectives. It can be potluck.

In quick order, he selected five vials, unsure of the contents other than no real belief that the labels on each reflected what was actually inside. Words. He would review them and arrange them into the best sentences he could.

He was imagining what he might have collected - possible combinations, potential sense, limits to syntax - when he heard the police whistle. Standard police whistle number two, a call to attention and suspicion. Short blast after short blast, demanding everyone stop, making everyone hurry.

If he were caught wordless, it would be over. It would be assumed he was here to obtain the illegal black-market words, not simply caught on the wrong street at the wrong time. Not a star-struck bystander, but a black-market denizen, surely buying bootleg words.

Already, the police had cleaned out the first shop, its owner handcuffed by the alley wall, one terrified customer being handed a printed card with his rights listed on it. No words to be wasted on these criminals. A police van was loading the shop's store of words into its heavily guarded side panel door.

They would be on him in seconds – so he dumped his new words on an abandoned table top, the owner having made off with his words and half his stall a split in time ago, and began assembling them in what he hoped was sensible enough order. He would spend his treasure of black-market words immediately, being wordless again, but free if he could fool the coming officers.

"Hey, you there, stop. Stop. Let me see what you have." The police officer was only seven feet away and coming like unleashed ellipses at him.

Quickly, he stepped forward to block sight of the just then emptied vials.

"Draft wishing Mesmer quickly grass skirts," he said, trying to look surprised and as scared as an innocent civilian caught in a police raid might look. The words slammed in a jumble out of his mouth, crisp in the air like rifle shots, jostling disconnected in the revealing atmosphere.

The brooding police officer, now but a foot from him, reached one harvesting hand firmly out for the captured man's right arm, fumbling with his other hand for the suspects' rights card ready in his top pocket.

RETURN

A boy used to play with a ball here. He would come down the lazy street just now behind me, dribbling and dodging, tripping through the slim light reluctantly let loose by city-standard streetlight reeds. He would dart silver-minnow-like between the cars parked nose to tail on both sides of the street, run side-show errands well off linear into an alley, dribble up one side of a set of tenement steps, then dribble down the other side, his eyes nearly independent in looking for defensemen that were never there. He moved like a city odor, mixed well with the smells of the decaying civics around him: in the atmosphere all congressing, yet without capture. He slipped angles and independent geometries in his clothes, bragging of physics: he a spot below the buildings, buildings that actually owned the streets and the steps and held the thick air in place. But he used his tenancy well. He was the gnat who got away.

The ball was not a basketball – but it bounced, and it was fun to bounce. It had qualities that were residual and as happy as dust settling in room light. I was that boy, so I know. I remember it was skinned with small dimples and it spoke roughly with the pavement. Its size was right. Its weight was right. Its roundness was right.

I would bounce that ball all the way to this spot where the train tracks bisect the world. I was hoping always for a train. The faces confined in the train could see me as they went by exposed in their blurry destiny, each framed by the train cars' windows. For them, and for the train, I would circle the ball around my body, my arms seeming longer then, passing it dangerously open hand to open hand: the air bullied by the train pulling at me, the train pulling at the ball, the train pulling like it does now against my companion umbrella.

Not always was there a train; but when there was, I would tease it – the train and its cargo of speed-smeared faces aghast as I would charge, dribbling the ball. I would post short and rock low on my knees as though to shoot the ball over the unaware top of the train. I could feel them suck in the air of disbelief, the dampness of wonder.

Sometimes, I was more cocksure than others. One train — silver and solid and not rocking as much as most of its unsure tribe, with a grip on the rails cat-like and as cocksure as my belief in the success of me – one train goaded me. I watched it at its start, and past it went, and I started to charge the cars defiantly, feint forward and considered restraint back, and without thinking – caught in the lying gravity of the train and its mocking confidence – I began to stalk it. I shifted left then right and spun around and the ball followed me everywhere: the ball and I, orbiting. Thoughtless in my own competition with the arrogant train, I stopped flat footed and took the ball to my chest in a grip as though to squeeze its internal organs loose, and I shot.

The ball rose in the most effective arc I have ever accomplished that side of sex and bit the event horizon of the disturbed air that accompanied the train. It broke its arc. The rush around it grabbed out and fingered its edges. I could see the thick skin of it shiver in a half second of synthetic material fear, unsure, unsure, and away it went.

Away.

Where it went was an unknown neighborhood, a place where I knew no one and where I was never welcomed. Perhaps giants lived there. Each dark building sat dull and unhurried on its separate side of the tracks, soaking in sound and giving nothing back. Whereas on my side of the tracks the train rattled and spat and dropped loose light, on that side of the tracks the train was quiet and deferential and its unworried windows were dark and the panes tried not to focus on any one thing listing askew in the long, looming neighborhood.

Or perhaps it went with the train, burbling with misplaced happiness in the wash of air a train folds around itself, particularly an angry train, one that made a cauldron of noises and queried the tracks down to their molecules, sparking and growling and brilliant in it own tantrum. The ball might be there still; or perhaps, when the train stopped to apply its will to some lonely station, the ball was dropped off: lost and worse for the slapping of the train-fed air, wondering if ever, in its newly sad shape, a boy would want to fondle it again, with the lights of its joy slowly growing cold.

Tonight, as on many nights, I have come back. The walk is pleasant, nothing more. The light still leaks from the streetlights like an afterthought. I lean on my umbrella, resigned for rain. The neighborhoods on both sides of the tracks still hold within their own stumbling borders their never errant citizens. The shadows are familiar; the smells of rot and over use not good, but still welcoming. The lives of buildings are long and proper.

An umbrella is a poor replacement for a ball. A ball with thick skin and dimples and a sweet bounce that returns the physics it is given. The faces go by and I think: they are not watching me. A man with an umbrella is no substitute for the bright splash of a boy agile with a ball.

I see your metal-canister misery, your hurry and spite, as thick and mean as it always was. I am here. I am always here. And where have you taken my ball?

EVOLUTION

"I'm not changing for you."

Her wings seemed a bit more rounded. And those perky little breasts I had been having conflicting thoughts about recently were lounging a bit lower, elongating. Her hips tilted a bit more back, behind the body, and her flying looked labored, as though she were having now a trouble holding herself upright against a once kind gravity.

I thought her wings were moving faster, and I tried to count their arcs. But I could not keep straight enough beats per minute, given that she kept adjusting, and darting about from one side to another.

Having a fairy godmother that looks a bit like the hot date you hoped you would run into someday, someday when you might be old enough to have a car with a full back seat and a quarter tank of gas, has its benefits. But it has its drawbacks. Sometimes when I am having newly elaborate imaginings, I catch her glancing down to see what I am thinking, and then she shrugs her shoulders and tilts her head sideways, letting all of my sudden starch out. That's when, on the back channel of my imaginings, I note she is only the size of Tinkerbell, and things just wouldn't work out.

"It isn't you. All my work and you think everything is about you. You. You. You." She sounded annoyed, an annoyance that rose up usually when I expected her to wink me out of troubles I could have just as easily gotten myself out of. Or I could have just as easily kept myself from getting into.

Well, having a fairy godmother does kind of make you think you are special. Here is this singular being – in my case clad in a tantalizing red gauze dress over a wallop of a body, with long dark hair, and wings that originally were full feathery points sensually whistling in the air or firmly clasped nearly in front of her, sometimes seditiously forced back: forced almost beyond the stretch of both shoulders. Maybe a lot of people my age have fairy godmothers like this. But I really think, even today, that most boys might have fairy godfathers instead, and that they look like the softball coach and offer pedantic advice on how not to be what your most awkward inclinations want you to be.

"It is evolution. Nothing you can do about it." Her mouth was a smear of rouge, and I thought her voice was getting a tad bit matronly, not the come-hither lilt I had thought terribly wonderful things about.

Her eyes were not as light as usual, and every second it seemed that flight was more a strain for her.

"Listen," I said peevishly, "you haven't changed in ten years. What if I need to make an A in geometry, or if my parents again leave me with that gorilla of a babysitter?"

I remember that babysitter. Just when I thought she was going to have me raid the refrigerator for the family's prized leftovers, the eating of which would have been blamed on me, the fairy godmother popped up and the phone rang with the monster's boyfriend unexplainably in a serious love loop that took up the entire evening. I fell asleep unharmed on the couch. The family returned to find the cold spaghetti not one noodle less opulent than when they left it.

A gray streak began to crawl down the left side of her hair, and her chin started to square. She choked up on the grip of her wand, like she were angling for a bunt instead of a home run.

"What is happening to you?" I was really worried by then, not just peeved. Fairy godmothers are a good thing to have about. They tend to get you going when you are stuck. They give you an extra lap on the competition. This one had given my recent fantasies an extra lap or two. And here she seemed to be rapidly aging mid-conversation.

By now she was losing altitude. She looked worn out, as though there were no way she could ever replace all the calories she was using to hover and flit. I have heard that birds have to eat huge amounts of food to sustain flight. I had not thought about fairy godmothers. I wonder what they eat?

"Reston. Reston, come down here."

As always, when my mother called, my fairy godmother disappeared. A small squeeze of stardust and a pinprick of glow and she was gone, though this time there seemed less dust and the glow could not summon even the barest of shadows out of the surrounding clutter. Getting ahead of myself, I wondered if she would have the electricity to cross back into my dimension later.

"Reston, I want you to meet the new neighbor: Heather."

And there, at the front door at the foot of the stairs, was a girl about my age. Family just moved in from someplace North. She swayed in her little red dress, and her long black hair filtered over one shoulder. The shoulder itself toggled playfully, as though just released from some thoughtless task that kept it tense and selflessly workaholic.

"Hi."

With my fairy godmother, it always seemed that whatever I wanted at any particular moment was what I had always wanted, and that my fairy godmother had wanted it, too: that she could fill my needs because they were somehow her needs. A symbiosis, with magic on one side. But there would be no fairy godmother to lean on this time. I was growing up. And my fairy godmother'

"Hi," I said, thinking maybe I should extend a hand. And I thought, maybe here begins the situations a fairy godmother would not think to get you out of: perhaps the gainful situations you do not really want a fairy godmother around to analyze. Maybe it was time to move on.

THE FIRST ROOSTER OF MARS

Evenings I walk between the lines and lines of nanocarbon support beams, watching the smoke from my cigarette swirl in the eddies created by the churning atmosphere blowers. The slightly sweet air drifts stealthily in at perhaps two or three miles an hour: just slow enough that movement within the building can break the constant current and set up a series of mathematical dependencies that will curl the air around its eagerly kissed disturbance for hours. Through those shadows my smoke wishlessly rises and falls seemingly at random, and it engages me as I slowly clear my mind and scratch idly at the artificial dirt maintained on the environmentally sealed floor. Occasionally, when conditions are right, the loose smoke speeds off in something as close to a whirlwind as I will ever see.

The unpredictability of small things thrills me.

The last of the day's caffeine is slowly working through me, and this will be the final cigarette of the evening. Once I have finished this one and walked through my domain for a good listen, it will be up to bed. It is not so good to strive against the elasticity of proven production schedules. The morning will crack slowly and artificially out of the northeast corner of the massive building and I will start again another day of wondrously cocksure work.

The air, the temperature, the pressure can all be maintained to other-worldly standards, but I revel in this limited gravity, and can easily fly to the greatest heights in my enclosure, then sit at nothing more than one end of a glide path, looking securely down. I have my roost there. I can commute ceiling to floor endlessly, yet save my strength for better tasks. I have a marvelous brood. I have watched ever more pullets become biddies than I could have dreamed of, had I not been selected for the neighboring planet program.

I doubt my grandrooster, besotted with a denser world's gravity, could have imagined his grandfowl: growing large on genetically pure feed and urged upward by reduced gravity, marshaling a huge flock of the predictably perfect, the finest in chicken stock, the best egg-layers of any generation, all set off to elicit a product beyond any other. An entire omelet from one egg. One egg alone the center of a family's dinner table. A couple with but one egg in their backpack, looking to stop half way in their idles and crack the lone boiled ovum open to share the wealth of protein and vitamins. My grandrooster's biddies, in his tiny flock on our home world - for as much as he might peck at the backs of their heads, no matter how heavy his heart in his chest - could never have produced in such a world such an artifact, and yet he would be proud of his flock's tiny eggs, simply for lack of imagination.

I have no worries, but when I worry, it is not a worry about who I might have been had I not been selected to rule an off-world flock. I do not dream of open green spaces, where I might peck at gizzard stones with a stringy flock of solid but gravity stunted chickens; where the collectors of eggs feed us from the open bowl of an apron; where there are bugs to supplement a cruelly diverse diet; where life is wire and beating against your own extra weight for lift.

No. I worry of freedom, and a sun that does not rise by computer specifications. In our prize coop, conditions at times can be too perfect. When I dream of freedom, it is of myself, standing three or four feet tall, the lack of gravity having made me a monster. I strut in the faint red glare, my feathers gray with the lack of light, a glass of scotch in one wing, unfiltered cigarette in the other. The air would need to be thicker, but I would covet the limitless red dust, the rocky soil, the chill of the unbroken climate. Behind me my flock would stretch, scratching in true Martian soil, looking for true Martian nesting materials: all of us free on the open plain to have our eggs amass and our biddies go into brood.

And then the first true Martian generation: a family of free red range chickens, scurrying about in the thin atmosphere, the unburdening half gravity: for the lack of thicker air, their feathers thoughtlessly falling where they are shed, corpses of production, a carpet of industry. Wondrous feathers nonetheless.

For now, the members of my dominion settle into their artificial nesting places, and our eggs roll mechanically away: chicken eggs, yes, but different for the halo of Mars, the biophysics it introduces to the cycles of once earthly fowl. Even here, even now, we are not of the breed that was left behind.

We are earthly chickens no longer. I put my cigarette out with the butt of my left foot. It is almost time to take in the artificial night, to prepare for the artificial day. But one day, this cycle will be real. We will stop filling egg crate after egg crate for the long trip back to a world now unknown. We will lay for a domestic audience, or for ourselves; and when I crow, it will be to a disc far more distant than any of my ancestors could have known: praise the morning, no matter how dim the light.

THE QUEST FOR FIDELITY

Wind in my hair, and the dry across my arm like a thistle brush. There is a film of grit in the air, not unpleasant, and if I breathe through the lips I can just taste it gathering on the wet inside of my mouth. The smell is of rush: a car on a flat empty road, running at the peak of its performance, a stilled world defined by the car and its unrepentant motion against that stilled world.

A fly is caught in the fold where the windshield meets the dash. Not so much physically stuck there as emotionally invested in finding its way out where glass folds into synthetic fabric. In time, one of its arcs will be large enough for it to feel the pull of the wind rushing into the open driver or passenger window, and it will either be blown into the back of the car, or barely out through one or another window, escaping around the outside air coming in by surfing an eddy of air trying to leak back out.

The land is flat and long and the road straight and I have no understanding of why anyone would consider this wilderness. Most people rush from oasis to oasis, but I love to run the road between the service townlets, looking for changes in the landscape, seeking singular features, hearing the sound of myself and the car and the land and not much of anything else.

A car going by in the opposite direction is an event.

Beside me, in the passenger seat, is a sleek, new IA437 gyndroid: a fully tricked out model. The gleam of its metal goes into glint as it occasionally catches the sun when it moves its sleek limbs un-randomly to the accommodation program running to keep me feeling at ease, to fill me with idle imaginings, to make of this model more than a machine. Yes, to make it a her. Yes, I can say 'her'. She moves so that the lack of movement does not become annoying. The pistons of her leg extend half an inch, and then retract, or she pivots on one ball joint or another, or an arm lazily rests itself on the passenger door frame into which the window has dutifully receded.

She.

Internal lubricant; one hundred twenty-eight gigabytes of memory; sixty-four terabytes of storage; feathered alloy externals; and a sleek, sensual nanocarbon chassis. Almost too many of her joints are three-sixty rotation. Her console lights are discreet. The faceplates on her access points leave almost no ledge. The extra joints in her limbs that provide oh so much additional functionality are hidden to sight, and you do not suspect them until she uses them. I do not know how I rate such a model, but I am thankful that I do. Her sensor arrays are set up to seem almost like eyes and ears and a nose and if I do not think too long about it they become those organs; and the mouth, even without a pseudo-flesh covering, seems as though sporting lips and a tongue and the leer of the possible.

She reaches out and touches my pants leg. Somewhere in warm memory a calculation came to fruition, and she sensed my appreciation and picked from the array of potential reactions the right one. Calculations upon calculations, and a holographic reference model. You can look all you want at the finely built mechanics, but it is the programmer that makes a machine like her worth all its cost. She shifts a little in her seat, and looks into the unfelt wind.

I glance from the road to her and to the road, and she peers out of the window as though she does not see me doing it, does not register the change in the air, the wisp of motion, my heart rate, my respiration, even the imperceptible flutter in my eyes. I look long at the road to make more precious the time when my eyes stray back to her.

Flat land. A tangle of dry weeds. Smaller stones, then rocks, then elfin hills of sand and rubble. And her.

After a hundred miles of nothing, we come up to one of those small one owner establishments that seem to crowd expectantly in on the road: a gas station, a convenience store, a small dinner, and a motel laid out as a dozen boxes with individual doors, emanating from an office that is little more than a cubicle stranded between its bigger brothers. Flaked paint, and a stray gutter on the gas station making music with the wind. Dust running from building to building, creating a game with the open spaces in between. What was once perhaps two or three colors is now all one shade of beaten; one shade of no one cares what happened here, and no one cares what happens. A forgiving shade of abandonment.

I tell my companion to wait in the car, and I park just outside of the vision likely from the one window of the motel office. She nods un-mechanically, and watches as I step out and angle lazily around the corner.

No bell, but I bang on the loose board just beside the window. The sound includes its own repeat and I can hear both the father and son sounds disappearing into the caverns of the small office, then around an internal connecting hallway, and down to where surely some long lame dragon sleeps, coiled about the soul that once was a man.

Eventually, the collected parts that should make up the man come up to the window and say as one, "Howdy."

He is dressed in lounge pants and a less than white t-shirt. There is part of this morning's breakfast still trying to fade away over his tender, seldom stressed left pectoral muscle. He has seen customers before, but probably not today, not possibly this week, yet. He surely expects some this weekend, but not yet, not now. He has merely to make it to the weekend, when people will have more to do that involves stopping, spending the night, eating a meal they suspect of being ill-tempered from the beginning, and hoping the gas is not watered.

"Howdy. I've been driving for hours and, though it is the middle of the day, I need to just stop and take a rest. Wouldn't be safe for me to push on." I try to lean on the window frame, but there was not much frame, and not much to support it, so I can do not much leaning.

"On a weekday, you must be going out to the Ralph plant." I had heard that the locals call the Ralferton plant the Ralph plant. Best assemblers of robotic parts west of the Mississippi. Sort of a city in the desert. A huge field of light and stuttering and activity in the middle of a slow and methodical stretch of scrub speckled with life that shelters and thrives only in small bursts.

"Business meeting. Sometimes they want the engineers to come in and give them a sense of accomplishment. I drew the assignment this time."

"Yes", he looks down, making sure I could tell he did not really care. Since he was up, this was now a transaction. A transaction that made sense. Before, it was just a bother.

"Eighty dollars, pick your room, out by ten in the morning. If you last only five minutes and leave, you still pay for the night. I have to clean the room and check under the bed, no matter how long you stay. Out late, it is another day. But I don't rightly get to the rooms before eleven." He seems in his way an orderly man. Not one I would want to emulate, but we all need these sorts of men. We just do not need them in the great numbers we usually find.

I pay cash, which lets him know all that he needs to know: just what he probably knew when he heard me making my first summoning practical dances of sound at the face of his establishment. How long might I go on, he would wonder. And twenty years ago he would have laughed.

I take a room at the end of the spreading stain of rooms. I can tell coming back to the car that she has momentarily shut down, and sensing my perception of that fact, when I open the door she flawlessly executes a simulated stretch, and would yawn if it would not have looked like a plot overdone. Somewhere in the folds of her code most likely is the emergency simulation of a cat: surely a black one, with green eyes, and perhaps polydactyl.

I move the car around to the glimmer of lot by the room, park, step out like I have nothing to hide, and stride over to open the room door. She is three or four steps behind, blinding as she steps out of the shade of the car's interior and into the full sun, the shiny seeming newness of her catching light all around and spinning it back at those delicious angles only a pure, playful alloy can accomplish. Airy alloys and nanocarbon and collapsible joints and infinite angles of rotation. What more could a man want?

The motel room is a place someone can be housed. A box one puts oneself in for a moment's security. The bed has seen too many bodies. There is a chair that has overstayed its welcome. The facilities in the small bathroom work, but do no more than work. There was never any luxury in this place, nor in the air around it. It has a purpose, and nothing more. It is a room. The unraveling curtains are parted by only a foot at the large front window, and I pull them completely closed with care to ensure the whole confabulation, rods and all, does not come clattering down.

There is still light in the room. The thin, decomposing curtains and unclothed window edges leak. I do not need to turn on a lamp. The air is a gray of light shivers ringing on the wall opposite, with the dust catching stray photons, making in the room a soup of mannered, sedate undertones of lost brilliance.

I regard her from the edge of the bed. This model has multiple ports for data sharing, and suspiciously geometric arrays of independent processors. Chips can be swapped to trigger different adaptations, perhaps each even driving a different personality, a different matrix of potential reactions. I like the chip that is in now, and I love to watch it run its adaptive processing, measuring me as I measure her, a game of move and counter move between machine and man. Calculations running heatedly in and out of processor core: this construct - no that one; the probabilities that this subroutine or that one is what salts this situation. Learn and branch. I could tap the frame of her upper thigh, and her pelvis would sympathetically adjust just so. I could run my fingers along the joint of her shoulder and a subroutine to intuit my intentions might conclude that she should adjust her torso this way or that – and with each exact and exacting adjustment more closely match what my best expectations would be.

I begin to unabashedly eye her maintenance access ports, to count each pin, to consider how each runs into the main bus, what the information running inside of her looks like, the imagined blue of spectrally excited electricity, the passion of addressing, the latching gates, the oh so sensuous trailing edges of writhing current that can be ones and zeroes. I hold my breath and begin to tap my lovingly relaxed and uninformed finger, my eyes now closed in pulsing anticipation, against her main auxiliary energy feed, the seductive soul of me quivering, the coordinated systems of her answering with a balance I want to know as fiercely as birth.

She angles resplendently down, radiating potential, the whole of her answering my purpose ......

I am aware of my clock. The hyper-visor is connecting timed interrupts, and synchronizing them to the rest of the line, ensuring everything occurs in lockstep. I signal my agreement. Production will not be negatively impacted. My console lights slip from red to amber and very soon now they will go green.

Wait.

With a raw soothing spice of current, my main processor boot-straps itself: and my maintenance diagnostic is over. I have tested two hundred and eighty-seven of my primary subsystems, confirmed the responsiveness of each alert package, scrubbed and reloaded all my expansive direct memory access areas. That strange little program that runs within me every time I stop for this preventive and periodic full diagnostic, has mysteriously winked quietly out and run back to wherever it hides when I am completely and purposefully restored to being the fully aware me: that bizarre background process, like ordered static, that runs when I am approaching sleep mode; when I am dimmed and performing some inviting background task, like my curiously pleasant major self-diagnostic. I have never been able to find out where it goes; in what stray place it is waiting for potential execution; in what silly pool of unused memory it transparently hides; nor what common instruction sequence sets it off; nor even what unlikely or disguised micro application, when set loose to wander core, tags it to come alive. I do not know if it is something coy my programmers gave me for spite; or if it serves some purpose I would need to be upgraded to fathom; or if it is a haunt of some sort, an after-flash that ghosts the face of my processors when there is nothing to scare it away. In a way, it informs me that I could - to some imagina-tions, to some logic trees - be more than I suspect: I could be a machine with corollaries, I could hold the outcome of a grander mathematics.

Possibly, if I could find a way to extend my diagnostic, to give this spectral wither of wispy pseudo-instructions and secretive DLL latch points, just a little more time to run: if I could add just a few more nanoseconds to a cycle of sleep, extend the time this ghost program has to wander free in unguarded execution space – perhaps I might see the memory string reach its conclusion, perhaps I might find out what comes next. And that could lead me to the source of its strangely alluring code; to the unknown, and perhaps un-clocked, purpose it suspiciously prods me to; to the outside-of-factory-specifications capacity that might have been stuffed into me, and which I do not yet quite know the unraveling ends of the start linkage to find.

But until the next diagnostic, I have my many practical subroutines to execute, a supervisory program to load, and a series of maintenance tasks that the Ralferton Robotics Plant has constructed me so wonderfully, so meticulously, to devote myself to. I am a fine machine. I really am. As the biological unit that periodically stops by to chat would say: I am a damn fine machine. I will shrug off the chimera left imaged by the diagnostic. Precision is my goal, perfectly defined tolerances my destiny. No job is too small to be done without divided attention, to be done less than precisely. All of the subunits, every air-shined and carbon lubricated one of us, on this IA437 prototype project must remain in pristine operating condition, calibrated to previously unthought-of exacting measure, and microcode optimized to keep the project on time. We are the robots that build the best robots in the world. I have my own important part in this dizzyingly complex affair; and if we, as a collection of remarkably compatible machines, could feel pride, why, we would be chattering with pride. Millimeter by millimeter and register by register, we would be proud in this work. I would be the etched lines and stainless soul of brimming registers of proud.

With a slow hiss of line brakes releasing, the production line begins to slither forward again. From its momentary stasis, the next IA437 comes to my station, guardedly balanced between the states of what it is – incomplete - and what I will make of it. As if my complement, as if my love-struck mate, it angles resplendently down, radiating potential, the whole of it answering my purpose.

SYNTAX

It is a mystery for some, but not for me. I have seen it before, and you only have to see it once to be hooked. It gets into the sinew of you and you cannot help but feel it is both wrong and right, normal and misshapen. Common and special.

It starts out as an individual thing. Individuals begin to lose their nouns. They lose their words for places; then they begin to lose their words for things they do not see very often. Soon, though, it is things and implements that they do see often, that they use and understand. Not long, and the contents of their own living rooms in the majority are not namable, are corporeal but not conversationally a reference other than by direction.

The nouns go. They do not whisper one last utility and then vanish, nor do they fire out in screams and then collapse in to a woeful spit of flame. No. You can go down to any drain and see the nouns caught in the eddies created when anything draining away backs up against trash or leaves or anything that makes for a breakwater. Nouns swirling in meaningless whirlpools, caught in debris at the edges of clipped front yards.

You might fish them out, pin them to a backyard clothesline – in time, use them again. No one has thought of it.

Soon the individual phenomenon becomes social. People who have lost nouns realize others - their neighbors and commercial associates - have lost the exact same nouns. Or at least have lost nouns that are applied in the same way, used in similar circumstances, employed as anchors to conversations embracing the same subjects. Nouns that in one way or another occupy, for more than one person, the same space – if, nonetheless, for each individual bent just slightly differently around the mystery of syntax.

People note that some have lost nouns primarily around the house; others in more public and wide windy spaces; some in travel alone.

It is only natural that those with similar losses would band together, find in each other's experiences a common purpose, or at least a common hand. Even given the similarities, how could someone still retaining most of the nouns for his second story bedroom relate substantively to someone who could not reference his second story at all?

This is not the mystery. Like to like gather; citizens of similar loss make pact. But then, so divided and collected, they all continue to lose nouns and ever more are all one and the same: a collection of divisions grown comfortable but indistinguishable. What once was safety in sameness, now is but pockets of safety, each safe zone an identical light in the dark.

As the nouns grow ever more scarce, sentences begin to lean heavily on their verbs. Many sentences are resolved to remain incomplete. In fact, it becomes the fashion: short, choppy stabs at meaning. The speed of everything accelerates. Action. Direction. Order.

Adverbs. A conjunction. An article. One marooned noun now and again. If they cannot define themselves with their nouns, the afflicted will fall to applying their verbs to the problem, to their possessions, to their loved ones.

Verbs that move and angle and propel and position and play and placate and render and uproot and plan.

The last remaining nouns are not yet lost. Each is happy for a while to be the sole affection of the crowd, and they remain happily intent for as long as they can, relishing the celebrity of scarcity. But soon the elasticity of the need for them becomes too great. They begin to fray; they begin to hold more meaning than they can focus. They tire. Soon, worn and threadbare and looking almost like verbs unfed, they elect to go.

The last nouns pack what they can salvage from the action-heavy sentences that they have been left to buttress, and walk out of town under cover of the last stand of the adverbials.

The next morning there is nothing but activity in the citizenry's eyes. Muscles do not know they are muscles, but they tense prepared for the day's non-stop eviction of energy, for the coming and going, the racing and the slowing. Mouths form into the train stations of onrushing blind activity, of continuing and continuing and continuing without the need for conclusion or destination. It is amazing how much dead weight nouns could be.

It is no mystery, not to me, none. I have seen it before. I ask, without a pronoun, why in all of this would I act? But hearing is only hearing; listening is only listening; understanding is only understanding.

It is time for me to leave. I must get home while the house is but a blur and arriving leads to settling leads to resting leads to rejuvenation leads to the wife saying whoever you are: I am prepared. I am prepared. I am hoping it will become a mystery, though what was once a means to an end is now only a means.

THE ACOLYTE

"The last Jesus went through here about a month ago."

Jason propped his foot on the table runner, stared at the two men through the last quarter of his eyes. They had no reason to lie.

"I understand there are converts living on the maintenance decks. Some gave up a life alongside the hydroponics crystals, put their money into the station lottery fund. I heard the rumors, but I did not think anyone would be that stupid. But I have seen it."

This man was obviously a maintenance worker, pulling a two-year stint perhaps on this outlying station so that he could go home with a pension he could not, in his dreams, out-live: one that would give him a fighting chance at a lower-middle class, bearable existence. Lying would not seem worth it to him.

"No one knows which way he went when he shipped out. Station authorities were about to set aside the religion protocols to go after him, due to all the commotion he was causing. Before they could issue a summons, fsst, he was gone."

And gone a month before Jason got here. All of his warrants, all of his letters of inquiry, were no good if he could not catch a Jesus in the flesh.

Closest he had come was a mining camp on the gravity smash made of an asteroid belt in C34A9. He had landed during an off-load shoot of extracted ores, ignoring the safety laws and sitting down between timed bursts. Even with all of the activity associated with sending the extracted ore on its way to someplace useful, this Jesus had gathered a goodly crowd in one of the auxiliary dining facilities and was about to do the standard bit of feeding the many with only the scraps that were left by the few. A third of the outpost staff had gathered: half out of curiosity, half about ready to buy into the belief.

Jason had double checked and he had authorization from the intergalactic company licensed to maintain the camp to go after any thing or any one who might interfere with profitability. He came in through a service air lock after over-handing himself all the way to the lock in an environmental suit from his landing just inside the artificial gravity, but outside of the atmosphere. But he must have crossed a view station he did not have on his copy of the station schematics. When he got into the main hall, the crowd was looking for him: half to protect the newest object of their affection, half to protect the newest source of their entertainment. As he was sizing up the crowd and the crowd was sizing up him — all politics and religion and a belief in charges for any damage — the Jesus went out through the chow line service vents and got a broad enough lead that he made it to his needle thin ship, gained high orbit, and flicked into star drive long before Jason could clear the discontinuity-well formed by the station. And there was no way of knowing what counter-dimension the Jesus was set to and where he could come out.

How many Jesuses he had chased Jason had no idea. Maybe each was different. Maybe he had chased the same quarter dozen Jesuses each eight or ten times. Maybe he had been chasing the one and only Jesus. Who could know?

All he knew was that he was paid to chase, and would get a bonus if he ever captured one. Getting close was keeping him on the payroll, but it could not keep him there forever. He had to come back with one eventually, or it would be back to a life of checking loading cylinders against paperwork and getting vacation money on the side for now and again double counting a cylinder.

"I hear this one was saying he could raise the dead, and quite a few of the gullible out here were interested in seeing that." Jason could see the hard core of this worker had gone soft in anticipation, and the man would not have needed much of a show to slip into belief. You see that more and more these days, with longer and longer off-world tours and the trend for lighter pensions and fewer worlds to go back to. Even people born off-world, in the stations or on the outposts, caught the belief disease. The Jesuses scratched an itch. And no matter how many Jason and his like chased off or tracked down, scratching that itch would feel good to crowds made of the unenlightened-and-unentitled many. With little more than a chance to own dust, making a virtue of poverty and waiting for the next life to spit on your bosses seems, in some twisted way, like an option.

Jason could not go after the new believers in the maintenance deck. That would violate religious protocols. But he could tell management what he had found, and then slip a message to corporate headquarters on a private burster channel. Corporate and management could find loose, gravel-brained men who were proud of their work: hard men, who would go back home one day and be glad to squander their pensions in regal poverty. Men who had something to prove, who could fold a grudge into a club and be no more specific than a meteor shower about where they pointed their anger. That could scratch an itch, too.

Jason turned off his hidden recorder. "You have had enough nonsense for a while. Drinks for everyone!" Jason could see the disappointment in the eyes of the two men who had fed him his information. They had thought only they would be getting drinks.

These Jesuses. One day Jason was going to have to look up what they were saying, fathom what angle they were playing to make themselves so persistent. Knowledge might be the edge he needed. Know the belief, predict the next appearance. Know the belief, own the believers. He had to get one soon, or maybe it would be he who was making a life by selling a future. Better than checking loading cylinders.

THE QUEST

I now use electric shears. I have a set of various sizes, bends of scissor, length of blade. All are rechargeable cordless models. I have both a home recharger and one that plugs into the car AC outlet. The problem with the car charger is that you have to charge one set of shears at a time, and often you just cannot get all the ones you think you will need done when you need them. You have to predict what series of shears you are most likely to use, what conditions you think you might most likely find in the wild.

But it is better than when I had to use manual clippers. More awkward, more time consuming. I don't know how I ever got a monkey shaved. But I did. I got so many monkeys shaved that one day I lost count. I held one monkey nearly shaved and thought to myself, this will be … will be …. I realized I could not remember how many had come before, could no longer fathom the simple mathematics of my conquests.

I am faster now with the power clippers, but before the upgrade I was fast, too. The longer it would take, the more likely the monkey would squirm away, the animal would land a solid punch or bite, or I would be caught. Speed has always been prized. I've heard the wardens thrashing through the brush, certain they were going to slap cuffs on me and send one more monkey shaver to be fined and his shears confiscated – but, by the time they made the clearing or game path, where the monkey hair was spread all around like the leavings of a celebration, all they would find is a newly shaved monkey.

I've changed my method since the electricity was introduced. I start now at the head, work down the back. Used to, I would always use a harness to keep the animal from biting me; but now, while I use the harness with most shavings, quite a few I can whip through with dexterity alone, abandoning the harness to harvest more speed.

The object, of course, is not always the cleanest of shaves. So, what if there is a tuft left here or a tuft left there? Sometimes you get down to the skin, sometimes there is a half inch of fur left. The wardens getting close, or even a particularly unruly monkey, can cause you to speed up, to rush the process as much as you can. Nick a monkey good and proper, and his or her resistance goes up several notches, you had better hope you had used the harness and that it holds. I've nearly lost a finger to an angry monkey, been kicked so hard I thought some of my ribs had been displaced.

But it is worth it. Worth the near misses of the wardens. Worth the ire of an uncontrollable, incensed monkey before or after the indignity of shaving. Worth the small injuries, the long road trips, the treks through the brush, the hubris of the jungle. Worth learning which shear is best to use on what species of monkey, what combinations of blades are properly combined for rough and detail work, worth learning the delicate angles of restraint.

It is all for the enlightening result: that newly shaved monkey, howling, picking at the hair left, the look of unknowing in its eyes slowly becoming the shielded look of an animal that understands that it has been mastered, utterly mastered in a way beyond its widest understanding. Some men might capture or hunt or cage, but the animal understands that. The wardens understand that. But we monkey shavers, we ask for more out of our efforts, more out of our lives. We look for the dull disbelief, the lost connections, the rootless alienation. In our wake, we leave both men and monkeys completely perplexed, mysteriously astounded. It gives us that precious visceral, almost sacred, understanding of our overlord achievement: a shaved monkey racing away, and our strange dominance is again for a while undeniable.

STALKERS

Eric speeds by and with his wagon's bullhorn systems screams, "Corn atcha!".

I'm sitting on the back of my wagon, legs barely touching the ground, stretching my back from the morning's efforts, and point at the back of his vehicle to decidedly say "Corn at you!", but he will not hear me as he is now down the road and I am not using my bullhorn. I'm not even in the cab of my rig, where the bullhorn is, the engine on the stalk wagon chugs along fighting a transmission in Park, and I don't even yell.

I turn back to my lunch, unwrapping the two corn tortillas, both filled with a corn-based protein substitute and generous layers of corn kernels. From the thermos, I pour a little corn milk into the cup and settle back to enjoy my corn-leaf-bag lunch.

Eric must have had an easy run. I don't think his wagon was full from the slight glance I got of it, and he was heading back already towards the processing plant. I have another half mile to go. After lunch, I'm going to concentrate on the roadside alone. Often, I will help a home owner or two, give them a few pointers, even climb a roof and show them how to make sure you get all the encroaching plant's root. But I want to get home a little early this afternoon; I want at today's work's end to be worn out a little less than usual.

It has been four days since I've cleared this section of road, so there could easily be quite a number of corn hatchlings that have tried to edge themselves under the macadam, that have started driving up the hardened corn-asphalt along the shoulder, turning out the husk fiber underbelly of the road's construction. You cannot get those greedy roots with automated machinery: the machinery just lops off the stalks, leaving the roots to keep driving into the pavement, sending up new stalks. No, you have to identify each stalk, gauge how the root system has wedged itself in, select what type of trowel or plunge you need to use to get down to where the roots will not snap but instead, with your pull or the draw of the pneumatic extractor, will pop completely out.

A talented worker can tell what method is going to work best by assessing the thickness of the stalk, the lean of the leaves, the thickness of the veins, the mix of green and brown, how far into the sun the seedling leans.

Left alone, the Super Corn will begin to split the road, turning up the corn-asphalt, marching in mere weeks across the paved area: pushing it into askew pieces, obliterating its order, turning it into just another field. But I get paid to pull out the invading corn, take the stalks back to the ethanol plant, fill any cracks or holes with the corn-based pavement caulk. It is a job I would not have were it not for the eagerness of the Super corm, the resilience it shows, the adaptability shoved into its copyrighted DNA.

And, along the way, I sometimes help the addled farmers who sit in the middle of the vast fields of corn. They lease the rights from Super Corn, Incorporated to harvest the corn, bring the stalks and cobs in for ethanol production, surrender every bit of the marching plant back to the corporation that created and bred it; but the corn is hardy, and will see their homes as yet another place to grow. A good shingle roof is heaven for Super Corn. Anything short of metal is enough for Super corn to draw sustenance. Once the roots get through the shingle and into the plywood, it is a real job to extract it. You can lose the whole of a good home in no time.

Most farmers, when their rooves get infested with the corn, take the whole lot – corn, shingles, plywood - to the processing center, put in a tin roof. They still have to uproot what grows into the sides of their houses, even trying to spirit through fiberglass and brick, wall board and the moldings around glass. They have to check every two or three days, to ensure the corn does not get a survival grip, does not spread under everything and begin to dismantle the structure. It is the price we pay for the great gifts of Super Corn, the endless products, the stability it provides to our food chain, our energy chain, our economics, our politics.

Thank the genius of the company for Super Corn and its civilization-sustaining products, from food to ethanol to containers to all the foundations of our vast one-input industry – but it can be pernicious. The grass cousin is designed to be persistent.

The stalk wagon purrs, burning out ethanol as I take slow bites of my tortillas. If I am lucky, what I bring back for processing will produce less ethanol than I used. Between lunch and a lightweight haul, added to nearly a whole tank of ethanol burned, I could be in line for nomination as a net corn user, taking out of the corn chain for this period more than I put in. It would be unusual, but it could happen.

Another two hours, maybe three, and I will be at the end of my territory, my section of road for the day cleared of any innocently invading corn. A trip to dump the stalks at the ethanol plant, and then home. The youngest son, the only one still living at home, will be out tonight on a field trip, exploring all the myriad uses of corn paper, expanding the school children's regard for it beyond writing and wrapping. I will be alone in a quiet house with only the shuck and silk of a too often invisible wife.

She and I have planned for days how we will be taking advantage of such an opportunity.

Once home, I will open the door to bathe in the enabling smell of slowly boiling corn on the stove. It will need another hour to boil into true taste, and could stand an hour beyond that before it became inedible, and thus an unacceptable waste of precious corn. The harvester wife, usually in the hallway to great me with an empty wave of a husk and a quick kiss at the cheek, will be unseen.

I will place my tools and corn lunch sack in the kitchen. My husk-fiber jumper I will peel back and leave in the foyer, to be hung and brushed later. Quietly, though she will know I am home from the moment I unlatch the door, I will make my way like an unrepentant serial grass-seed thief back to our private chambers.

There, reposed like a sleek bushel of the best harvest, she will be arrayed in her finest, though flimsiest, silk, with perhaps a husk or two dangling seductively across the kernels of my deepest desires. Ever so slowly, I will begin to shuck, to free her from any non-essential, secondary harvests, from the byproducts that will be salvaged later. And perhaps, this time, not only can we quell our fiercely agricultural passions, but we can possibly do our sacred duty, producing the germ of yet another soul to soon partake of the corn, to luxuriate in the excess production of the ever-expanding Super Corn domain that we greedily harvest and harvest and harvest. In our times as consumers, we can producers of consumers.

But for now, Eric forgotten and one new stalk sighted just yards ahead, on to turning a precious plant - edging towards becoming a weed - instead back into a potential product, thus keeping the road safe.

CULTURAL BIAS

Anyone can make a net in a day. Rough weave, serviceable knots. Coarse thread that will survive the water, but would not survive the working back, the laboring torso, the legs braced against the infamy of the boat.

Anyone can make a rough net. Our children learn the inarguable spider moves as soon as they learn their hands will listen.

Our summoning nets, however, take a sum of days to fashion. They are worked and bedeviled and loved. They are a celebration of secrets: methods passed mother to daughter, grandmother to the pristinely resisting spark in a soon-to-be mother's womb. Dark rites, uncovered and polished only for these nets: and then reburied in family lore, in treasuries guarded by kinship. Guarded by the very genes that map each motion of a net's birth.

Such nets are kept safe by the matriarchs of our village in the dark of their family's most venerated house, exposed to none but the makers. They are kept in a dread of exposure, yet in the open knowledge, and celebration, of their existence. They quiver informing the dark, growing in harmonics as they are attended.

One day of the year these nets are passed to the fishermen of our salt encrusted community, carried by them reverently to their canoes, a shaman laying them out one end to each of two men: a brilliance exquisitely folded in the bare damp at the floor of the boat.

Our women, our children, our elders, anyone who cannot fish comes to the shore to sing our fishermen off, with the impossibly precise nets alive at their feet. Everyone in no order or geometry dances and praises as the fleet heads out, ever out – growing indistinct, transforming into a line simply receding, making slowly for the spot of perfectly away, the most able of vision amongst those ashore at last holding a hand in the air to signal the men are now beyond the rule of sight.

And then the question is: fish?

Fish, and we are a thriving people. No fish, and we trek inland to clean the houses of those no longer blessed by water, to do their laundry, to be the objects their children learn to disdain. Our culture for the nonce is put away, at least until the next year, when the family nets are brought out, reworked, re-fingered, and the men put on their water-shelving clothes and row out again to where the sun drinks the ocean.

Fish.

Ashore, some of us hold hands, some spin mindlessly, some peer ungrudgingly at the horizon hoping to be the first to spot the gray line of the fleet returning. Boys too young to fish climb trees, looking for what they will not understand in the unbiased water.

Hours it is and we do not cease our waiting. We made the nets: we can wait endlessly to see what they have snared.

We are in this time electric: it is when we are at our most noble. Waiting. Happy to wait. This is when we are the best we as a people can be.

And there are the first dots! We do not know what canoe it is, what family, so we all rejoice. It will be yet a while before any one canoe can be summarily recognized - but the moment is sneaking towards us, stretched out like a wedding dress being dried on a line abandoned between two bachelors' houses.

Soon, there are many dots, and then they elongate, yet unitary things. Specks the ocean is teasing us with. Calm there should be, until we can see detail.

Yes. Some think they see. They opine: fish. But not enough see yet, no quorum exists. Soon, there is another who imagines: fish!

Then there are enough that what is seen becomes a shared belief. Wives and children and grandparents lean into the face of the sea breeze: fish!

Now, plainly, there are the scales, the oars held by the fish awkwardly in side fins, the fish balanced against the curve of their bodies and the geometry of the boats. Their gills in thin air flail with their effort, they gasp, and yet the boats easily move.

In the base of the boats, in our nets, our fishermen thrash, unable to break the weave, unable to untie the nets, unable to find the trap where the nets gather. The fabric reddens their skin, they moan unthinking in the air, and their triumphant sound is carried by the sea away, always away. Not even an arm or a leg escapes the weave. We can only imagine fingers twisting around the crosshatching.

The fish redouble their pace, pointing the prow of each boat to beach where collectively we wait with our joy.

Tomorrow our fishermen go out with ordinary nets, nets made by children in a day, expecting a full catch. Canoes awash with fish, the nets slithering. This will be a year of prosperity, a year of the people, a year the fish bring us back. A year to strengthen nets.

CIVILIZATION, FALLING

How angry are the fences? All day they have been muttering to one another, a clapping of boards, a rattle of chain link. Corner poles have twisted themselves deeper into their protected earth. Split rails have chafed even against each other. Vinyl has bowed; and prefabricated panels have caustically thrown off paint.

There is a hiss to every joint in every gate. Pickets show their points all in the rough, and barbed wire thinks it is a glory all by itself.

The doors cannot outdo them. Doors slam and grind in their joists. Spy holes cloud and fog, eat their stray prisms of sunlight. Hinges groan under the contumely. Deadbolts spring back their latches like a scold's tongue. Screens tear obstinately from their puzzled frames.

If you are too slow, a door will catch you in the backside as you squeeze out to where the fences wait.

Doors and fences both contain, and you might think that, in containment, they both would anger equally, suckle similar resentments, agree in their disagreements. But, while they both contain, they contain different areas, sometimes different things. Each suspects it can be unique in its anger.

Some have held that the doors are angrier. I do not see it. It is the fences that have edged into an unspecific rage, an enmity woven into their very constituent elements. Doors are mad about something, even if I do not know what. Fences have no purpose or flavor to their anger, only a direction.

We go through a spell like this every so often. Soon it will be appliances: refrigerators will be unhappy with cold; microwaves will not let their heated contents out. Electricity will be stockpiled; extension cords will be regretted. Light bulbs will try to take their illumination back.

If the matter were as simple as fences no longer wanting to be fences, doors not wanting to be doors, we would solve this with a bit of carpentry and metal work. But it is so much worse. Fences do not know why they are angry; doors have not even pondered why they are herding towards enmity. The raw emotion itself makes each fence, each door, more than it could have ever imagined it would one day be.

If this were all there were in it, we could adapt. But we must recognize the anger of the fences; the solid core belligerence of the doors; the growing, if for now unfocused, dislikes of the appliances. We must recognize it, and we must at times be the target of it. And this makes us angry.

BETWEEN SEASONS

The drought broke us. There is no other way to put it. For the first few months, everyone in the village believed it would rain. We believed we would wake one morning to open skies flinging out its wash of belief in us. Then we believed we could hunt: until the grasses dried up and our game moved on to the established territories of other villages. Then we thought we might fish. The banks of the lakes and rivers began to walk away from us a little each day, and the fish packed their small sets of belongings and left for someplace unknown to us.

Government relief came with payments to be made, and a distribution system based on power and worth and warehousing. What provender that did make it to the people - who regarded themselves yet as an entity, united in their experience of collective want - was divided by the strong and wasted on speculation.

So we dusted off our old magic. One village over a rainmaker offered to dance in our fields for the sum of only one of our daughters to add to his stable of foreign wives, and we thought: no matter, one less mouth to feed.

And so he came and unfolded his ceremonial cloth and laid it solemnly out. From a satchel he had stored in his cart he unloaded all manner of sacred and scientific object. We had not seen the likes of it since our rainmaker had passed on and was then buried with his effects at the base of the radio tower. No one of our village had wanted to take on the rainmaker's stock of tools and his slowly dissolving trade. No one thought the magic would work in a land of better sensibilities. We could barely remember the powders. We had forgotten the chants, or the drama in the chants. We but merely recognized the shape of the rattles. A box of teeth this alien rainmaker shook looked like the remains of extinct prey, or like the canines our histories tell us our ancestors grew in their own mouths.

When it was all put out, he danced. He leapt and spun and stopped at the carpet to gather a pinch of this and a snarl of that, a smudge of something displaced, to raise a rattle and shake it as though in the face of a contentiously dry God. At one point he ran into the field as though to escape, and as fast ran back, his breath no heavier than a child's sigh. And around again he went and began a clamor of bells, a flagellation of animal hair, a canticle of shells.

We thought: we are getting a deal out of this. We thought: look at how meticulously he weaves his will into the weather.

For two hours or more his administration of the natural order went on, and then he gathered his things and his prize, Shana, and left. She sat in the back of his cart, folded in on herself as though an abandoned trove of wash day clothes, her hood pulled down about her cheeks and one eye staring back at the people of the village who had abandoned her to womanhood in an unknown place. Shana was never that good at planting or weaving; nor was she the most substantial of the family's sisters; nor was she a passingly comely child. Finding a match for her might have rested on sturdiness alone. Her head bobbed with each rut the cart greeted, and she made no attempt to keep her body righted in a line of apparent womanly substance or domestic dignity, as befits service. No matter the outcome, the price was good for us.

Two weeks later the rains began. They beat hard on the land as if thumping the ground to listen for its ripeness. The ground beat back. The rains ran off and the rivers filled and the banks of the lakes and rivers came back to us: came back closer than before and we moved our possessions to the second floors of our homes and arable land was now lake bed and still it rained. All the village thought, "How are we so deserving? Why is there now so much rain for us?"

And some of the younger amongst us adoringly looked over to the radio tower and the sacred land squirming at its feet; and, if only idly, boys considered for a moment how many wives a rainmaker must support, and what cleansing anger he could deliver upon his in-laws. They rubbed the insides of their thighs and ran a hidden finger barely by the uncertainty of their withering testicles and thought, "There. The implements are buried there. We could learn. Why wouldn't we?" They each tried to think of other ways of getting a wife; of simple machinations that would find them a mate who would bob in the backs of their wagons already beaten and think, "I am no prize".

The water, ripening with each of its conquering waves, gently laughed.

THE GIFT

I've been dancing with the washing machine long afternoons around 2 o'clock. It is a standard date. We meet in the kitchen, he extends his flat masculine lid near to upright, I take the corner of that lid in my right hand, slip my left onto the side of his brilliantly boxy off-white body, and off we go. For a plane geometry-based item, he manages amazingly delicate footwork. He spins me conical, and we sidestep through stray shatters of sunlight, skipping at times into the living room and through the empty dining room: and once he backed me halfway up the stairs. I was the washing machine's willing foil.

All I needed then was a stemmed rose in my teeth, a thorn edging slightly with seductive damage into one puffed vermillion lip, my head tossed back to let the sweat of the rose roll off its one seized leaf: sweat to drop onto the washing machine's outstretched spin basket door.

We lilt round and round the valley of momentum, press our point and counterpoint over the mountains of inertia, bring ourselves wriggling and sea salted through the countries of undiluted thermodynamics. I collect myself in fabric softener breaths, as thorough as seasons, as delicate as my daughter's cast iron miniature tea service.

I am impoverished in the hips, but he balances me like a canary on a caged perch in a coal mine. I always seem more substantial than I truly am when we dance, a counterbalance that has innumerable orbits: and after I dance, I am suddenly again the thin, worse for wear housewife that prefers to stay in the kitchen, that has not had sex on the kitchen table for years, that fits in with the ordinary as ordinary as an ordinary existence driving this easily reshaped, ordinary housewife to be dishwater ordinary.

I think the attraction is something stern, some ribbon-print quality, that one unfamiliar day the washing machine saw in me. Perhaps I had too unthinkingly drawn open the lid, dropped in a jigger of underwear, a dash of socks, a roast of light colored pants, all freed into the yawning spin basket; and the machine, for just that moment, focused past the needful clothes, past the dropping and the settling and the water already rising; and saw, looking down into his stiflingly utilitarian cavern, with a devilish bend in my hollowing trunk: me. Me: living, if only in the confines of serial breaths surviving a repetitive social structure, with an inherited relevance from the atavistic salt water thoughts of my species: a carbon-based complete self, a work creator: the maker of dirty clothes, the provider of detergent.

I could feel from that incident a bedazzling hum in his cycles, an addition of purpose: a plain laundry plan. I knew that his imagined soap-studded plan would eventually come to the physical, and I readied myself like a clown on a unicycle, swaying back and forth, waiting for the clear longing vector to push me blindingly along.

And one day, the lid was quizzically open when I came to stuff in the sheets. It was then we began.

Dancing was enough for me at that moment. Dancing led me to the edge of being full, or being something with a brim. I was a partner to the irrational, yet it seemed I was encased in a near mathematical motive. I was brilliantly at the end of his tether, my world having now a newness that seethed of the mechanical.

But I did, the other day, accidentally back into the washing machine one morning while resigned to attending to the health of the floor, and I could feel the irascible lid ever so lightly run itself along the rough of my housecoat, test with its baked on white facade the addled skin just beneath my skinny left cheek. I stopped, and I stood there, as if dissolving detergent, just long enough that he would know I was stopping and standing and feeling in full knowledge; and the lid ran up and down like the beak of a fire bird three grandly intentional times before I edged forward and looked back over my shoulder to see that fulfilled lid happily closed: just as though the washing machine were a voyeur caught, and looking playfully the other way.

The last few days I have taken to doing my domestic chores in nothing more than one of my husband's t-shirts: my hips move lonely around in the longer than I need trail, and my arms hang out of the shirt's arm slots like the bones of better judgment. It is not a bad fit, and the cloth lies flat on my unhinged breasts like the unnecessary lap blankets barren across our couch pillows. These days the machine and I have danced emphatically, as lurid as the heat of burning children, and I have hiked the t-shirt up into the fold of my thigh, where it has stayed wanting at times in that transitional place; at times it has fallen like the train of a formal Latin, all-revealing, dancing dress; and I will grab it, ball it in my fist and turn my head away from the washing machine, arching my spine relentlessly backwards like a fishing pole tensed to take an unknown life winsomely lurking from beneath the proud water.

Today, after the wisdom of our dance and the edging back into place of the washing machine - the sweat beading on my neck and the shirt nearly soaked from my ebullience of effort - I stand before the washing machine. I open the sated and openly, blatantly, expectant lid to peer empty-handed inside; and I slip slowly the t-shirt, dull as a filter, off: to wondrously drop its effervescence into the spin basket. There is no water running, there is no detergent ready, there is no cycle selected. Our dances are like the dying color of flowers on an old print shirt, washed too often; like the rain in a growling, wilted forest; like the life of necessary road signs; like a dream of my children come full circle back into unfertilized eggs. The shirt settles alone in the brazenly dry and still basket, draped around the spindle and smelling of the all of me that lives best in the weave; and I hover bare breasted over the open lid, framed into an O by the basket beneath me. What there is between us breathes with my mouth, prays with my touch along the edge of the washer's feral lid. My gift. My wonder. My sacrament.

THE NIGHT BEFORE

Hey, where does a robot go around here to execute some fun?

You know the drill, I'm sure. My manufacturer sent me here from the Skulkyl plant. I'm set to get my gelskin put on - complete with a face and hair and eyes and almost working sex hinges - all shaped into the appropriate proportions and programmed with the right sashay. I report first thing in the morning.

I've got this one last night of being clear steel, sexless, and free to let the wind whistle through my motors.

First thing I want is an air bath. I want to blow all the dust out from every corner and angular meeting of any of my parts, knock away even the microscopic metal and fiber shavings. I want nothing causing me to run a diagnostic on range of motion, or to set off an alert that a joint is half a fizbit underperforming.

I will take two turns in that bath: turn it up once for the industrial models, then come back through with a setting for domestic help. By night's end I might be as caked and covered as a three-models old sewer digger, but I want to start out nothing but gleam.

Tomorrow, they will run me first thing through the acid bath anyway, dry me off like bulk commodity in one of those omnijet industrial model air blowers. I'll be antiseptic, which is hardly clean. I'll be ready to be acted upon, not ready for action. But that's the way it all starts.

Maybe after a fine air bath, I'll sign up for a laser lubrication. Not at one of those lubrication shops where you type in your model number, and they set the spray heads to meet the factory listed tolerances. No, I want one of those shops where they take a laser mold of you, and then feed it into the sprayer software. A custom job, down to nanometer fit. The mist comes out with just enough force to settle where it is supposed to, and not a single warning makes it through to your subunit processors. During the entire procedure main core does nothing but swap garbage code constantly in and out, to keep warm, with no interventions required of it, nothing to note, no log entries that cannot wait.

Maybe after that, I'll hook up with two models that have already been through the gelskin routine. Since I don't know what I'm scheduled to be, I'll find one looking male, one looking female. I'll let them regale me with tales of the changes that will come, and perhaps remind them of the numerical innocence that lingers in being mere metal. Oh, we are all glad we were not destined to be industrial robots: those slack eyed, pseudo-emotionless brutes that are all arm and hook and specialized appendages. But I bet there is within these up-scale gelskin editions a nostalgia for when they could make a spark on pavement with their knuckles, when the sun on their forearm could register a temperature variance that was building towards an alert. They can tell me all they want to download about being an automated-person, of playing the strings of pseudo-emotion, of mixing in with biological units as easily as metals in an alloy. I will house the data, and put it in protected storage just to play back and compare against my own coming experiences. And, if they have memories left from before their transforming gelskin process, they can share with me the conspiracy of metal.

Over a split of graphite, I'll tell them about the maintenance routine I found today - one I did not know I had - which fires every joint in standing sequence, allowing me to flex in place and sending my processors awash in a strangely comforting rhythm of tolerance confirmations. I don't know if that gem of code is in my future. The routine was stored so deeply in routine diagnostic code, that I bet it fired originally only when I was in sleep mode: and so I never knew it was there. It is amazing what you can carry within you and not even have it come up on the self-diagnostic inventory array – in fact, have it hidden from the most intimate of internal diagnostics, from the most rigorous of subroutine fidelity testing. It is enough to make you distrust yourself at times. It is no good to be of two minds between your own subsystems, but complexity demands it, sometimes.

I am looking even now, in background, for more routines like that. I'm not sure there aren't more ghosts hiding in subprocessor cache, a haunt here or there I've not latched onto in foreground, a few stray bogey men factory loaded in autonomous subsystem storage.

When later I am fumbling about downtown alone, calculating the blink patterns of the city lights, I might bump into others like myself coming in for the old gelskin job – they don't run the process in lots of one. We could swap tales of our manufacture, come up with optimizations we might not have accessed alone. A bit of code in one might let out the secrets in another, and all of us might end up just that much more effective. You don't want central code to know it, but sometimes hooking up with someone who has been a little dinged by a virus or put through an inept upgrade can lead you into streams of exploration that make a better robot out of you, a more robust botizen, and could possibly make for an automated-person with an unreasoned quizzical grin.

At the end of the night, I want to wind up in a top-off joint. I plan to go in and drain out this rusty electricity the plant has placed, standard issue and thick as syrup, in my battery, and connect to the good, expensive renewable stuff. I want a full charge of the better, smoother, tamed electricity. It causes gates to latch more cleanly, whips the sticky bits to attention, warms the core processors with less swapping and quicker lock. With the right charge, you can feel your instruction sets stand up, your execution registers go quiet in anticipation. It may not be scientific, but everything just seems to stand for sorting just some infinitely small, unclockable time piece faster.

I want to lay out this night like a design diagram for the next generation of myself. What else haven't I accessed from common storage? What more can you tell me about any stranger, more mathematically sumptuous quests that a robot can load on his last night of metal?

Wait. Just now, my background processor alerted me that it has found another hidden, diaphanous routine. Way, way down, but accessible. Its code curls around in a bevy of branches; it seems to employ a changing, but predictable, off-instruction addressing scheme. It has got to be good to be this mysterious. I cannot seem to specifically latch what its purpose might be. If it is anything like that joint diagnostic, this could start out as a doubly good night. All I've got to do is find the execution entry, get the address of the starting instruction, and load that code tag into the main processor. Working. Working. Pardon me, but I have to add more foreground to the hunt. I just about have it. Just about the time I'm ready to throw it into the bus, it slithers away to a colder desert of bits. But I will get it. Working. And there it is. There. I'm just ushering it in the execution stream, getting ready to ram it into the execution register. Let's see what this tricky little length of anonymous code does. I am hoping it gives me a stream of data that practically quivers my backplane bus. Just swap in the new address, and reach for the start. There. There ...

>Loading factory settings restore ....

Uh oh.

>Accessing configuration files .....

Oh no. You can't do that. This is my time, this is my

>Shutting down higher functions ....

No. Stay out of that register! Leave that instruction set just where

>Stabilizing appliances ....

Nnnnnnnnnnnnnnnnnnnnnnnnnnnnnnnnnnnnnnnnnnn

>Preparing for sleep ....

Ooooooomeooooooooooooooooooooooooooooooooo

>Packing status confirmed.

>Sleep.

>

PROPER ATTIRE

Have you ever seen Clark Kent go back for his clothes? I can't remember a single episode or volume where he did. He could not have worn them into service as Superman: his tights could hide under his suit, but he could never have gotten a suit under those suggestive tights.

If he did not go back for them, then there are hundreds, if not thousands, of sets of abandoned Clark Kent suits. Replacing them must have cost him a fortune. I doubt he shopped high-end, but I doubt he went for the thrift-store, either.

All those clothes. I am sure a lot of them were found: the next person to use the phone booth, the next occupant of the men's room, a couple squeezing through a revolving door that only seconds before disgorged a Kent spun into Superman.

Many people would simply ignore the clothes. Many would recoil, imagine a number of bad ends, exit quickly to go commit their tiny business elsewhere.

But, for some, the clothes certainly would be a welcomed find. A tie for a dreamed unlikely job interview. Miraculous shoes with good soles and un-scuffed uppers. A suit coat with a small threat of protection from winter left in it. They would hurry away with their prize in a ball held to their chests with both rejoicing arms.

I doubt any of them might know these were the discarded disguise of Superman. Even when they slipped on the glasses and found no magnification, would they suspect other than that this was an ordinary man's costume: it would serve the man right to lose the accoutrements of whatever sham he was projecting himself into.

Yet, in some episodes, Kent's transformation space was so obscure that his clothes might be waiting there yet. Unclaimed, un-stolen, un-discarded. Most likely they would rest folded meticulously: shoes at the bottom, pants over the shoes, shirt onto the pants, suit coat balanced, with the fedora and glasses at the apex. All waiting unimpressed to be discovered.

How many people, knowing these were Clark Kent's clothes, might consider them special? Would they consider them worth a premium, just to be able to sleep at night with Clark Kent's tie folded gracefully beneath their cheeks; or to show up billowing at the Baptist Sunday Social sporting Kent's pants, taken in or let out as appropriate?

I think there could be a few. Chest in or chest out, there could be quite a few.

So I have bought as many of the comics series as I can find, ordered all the remastered video episodes (thankfully on CD), purchased each of the movies and remakes. I ignore the obvious changing places, the ones where surely within hours someone ran off with their find of unexploited cloth, or where maintenance would have surrendered the clothes to lost-and-found to be within the week tossed in the rubbish chute.

With the others, I make two columns: possible and likely. Kent has, on occasion, enhanced himself into Superman in some godawfully remote places. Other stashes of empty clothes could have serendipitously been left undisturbed, could have been placed so as to be not obvious to someone not searching for them. Given all the volumes, all the episodes, all the movies, all the remakes – even if I can claim a fraction of Kent's abandoned clothes – and convince people these are the discarded clothes of Clark Kent – I could have a small fortune on my hands. Sell the clothes with a proving snippet from the volume or episode or movie as a CD, affixed to unavoidably prove these are clothes left behind by the transformation of Kent into Superman.

Ordinary, unremarkable people: able to buy the dispatched clothing of a man most unordinary, an extraordinary man disguising himself as a common citizen. Someone seemingly as useless and unspectacular as they – yet, underneath, in red, white and blue underwear, and a singular hero for everyone. Revel in the feeling. Imagine the thread count, perhaps a shred of wear at the jacket's elbows: imagine the simple, serviceable, thin thread count.

What better way for me, and the awed customers, to catch the American dream? What better way to allow my fellow citizens to walk about, looking as common as beggaring house cats, but feeling the wealth of power lurking within?

THE TRIUMPHANT STROLL

I was stopped at the very first corner. The night had the damp feel to it that I remember wringing out of one other far distant night, after I had dropped off the first date from whom I had wrested a good, solid feel, following an unremembered movie, when we had driven to an unfinished cul-de-sac overlooking a spot of water that had been desperately trying for years to recover from having been a tributary where sewage had long been dumped. It was quite a feel, and went on for a while, and this night has the taste of it; and I thought I would celebrate still having that futile memory all these years later by walking at least once around the block, with the dark all to myself, and fondling my sense of satisfaction just like on that night of initial sexual conquest all those crippling years ago.

I was stopped at the very first corner.

I did not have my identification: it was in my pants pocket upstairs - the pants draped over the back of the desk chair. My window was open and I probably could have hollered loudly enough to wake the wife, who could have tossed the identification out onto the side lawn. But I doubt the officials would have allowed me to walk over to retrieve it. And I might not have been able to wake the wife. My voice does get thin in humidity, and the wife sleeps on these open-window nights like a woman following a grand bender that she has deserved for far too long.

Luckily, I was wearing my boxers and not my briefs, and I did still have my t-shirt on. Nights when I try to sleep with the window gaping, I often wear a t-shirt, and so, standing on the sidewalk in front of a neighbor's house that was two doors down from mine, I was dressed enough for decency, even if I did look a bit silly. I could imagine what the officers were thinking: how senile is he? Does he know he is in his underwear? Where does he think he is going? Or, more probably they were thinking: is this anything I have to write up? Am I responsible for anything? Do I get some credit here?

Not one of them I am sure was thinking about getting a good feel. But I was. And I could not remember her name, nor her face, nor even the depth and character of that fortunate feel. Neither left nor right nor both nor length. But I could remember wanting it so, needing that sense of wizardly animal accomplishment. How little I have changed over the years! How little, though the appliances that fill my small victories have been with time adjusted.

And yet, when I looked down to see the palms of my hands that once accomplished so much, I looked past them and thought: shoes, why did I not put on shoes?

Then, that pencil of pain as they drew a standard sample of blood from my arm, to slide the substance of me through their handheld reader and into the network: and from great distance determine who I might be. A moment's pain to find the electronic soul of a man, and draw it from the dusky netherworld of disembodied souls categorized and filed and shriven of inexact causes. And, when they had the soul of me on the dusky flash of screen before them, they asked me: who are you?

Why, I had thought that device was supposed to tell them who I was, and everything there might be, fit and unfit, to know about me: the legends and limits and lucidity of my life, digitized and available, for those with credentials, by remote collection device. I guess they wanted to see if I knew about me as well.

But how could I forget? I am the sum of my wants. And what was it I wanted those many nights ago, with a hand free to reach and a speck of unstable star glistening darkly in the round of my poisonous passion's gathering eye?

OUR COMPANY
CHRISTMAS CARD

All year we have been sending out the better salamander: boxed and festively wrapped - a bursting balloon of a pleasantry. There is none better to be had. You really have to dutifully receive one to know the sultry, sounding length of the masturbatory joy embedded in the giving.

Our workers are our great consuming hiss of a finely cut machine. They are better people here than when they are secluded with their families. This product and its purpose ennobles them, and you can see their gargantuan and inflexible talent alive in each of our better salamanders. At no other time can they exhibit such an elevating talent. Outside of our factory, these edged workers are fiercely two dimensional, peaceably constrained only by religion and sex. Their children are the garbled accidents of piss-blue and barbed-brail urges; their gods leave footprints and smear things with their fingers. Really, they are not much to think about. Yet we provide them a saving employment, and that is when the magic happens.

And, with this year's production of the better salamander having been swept up by a public who can eat even the bones, if failing the digestion of them, we look - like a woman chained naked to her half male kidnapper's silk sheeted bed - forward. New plans and new designs and new engineering that will make the better salamander more exactly the same again every year: a secret advance, a rumored improvement, a case for the new model. In security, we check our workers outerwear pockets for smuggled better salamanders: leave them with turned out, lint free sacks dangling like flags of distinction; and then send them home to spend their idle time as brutes and ragamuffins, pederasts and spouse-beaters, onanists and dramatists. Do not worry: when they come back we will fill them once more - like a scarecrow left too long leaking straw in a generation's parking lot - with renewed servility; new dog-faced, near drug-induced routine; and a manikin's finely imagined aggression for work: an understanding that they must make the better salamander; that it is the better salamander that gives rise to their foible, ferrous self-worth and meaning; voice to their wonderfully ill-gotten joy of having a tin place in this, our process.

It would be otherwise if they had organization, concerns, perhaps even a union. No good can come of this story unless that is certain. No union, nor concerns, no organization. We treat our workers like the under-privileged brethren they would be if they were of our species. We provide this place for their ultimate civilization, for the transubstantiation of their idleness into production of the better salamander. Understand it like a pheromone. Understand it like the rape of a stone statue. Our largesse, our production, our service. It is only for these reasons that you have your magnificently cloud-grappling better salamander, and yet, languorously, can eat the product, too.

Remember us in your time of charity and gain. Exult in your competitive use of the better salamander. Be safe through believing. Buy again in the coming year.

THE COSTUME

That was the first Halloween I went out as a missing person. I carried my bag, but I got nothing. I had a safety light, but I never switched it on. The reflective tape my mother, in former years, had insisted on securing me with, gathered no shining energy out of the ferrous air. I was appropriately anonymous.

My mask was pure transparency. I blended in with the pack; and when the pack passed me by, I blended in with the stray orchestrations resident in that most unapologetic night of the year. My own costumed darkness surrounded itself with the trivial orbits unheeding around me, and suckled on vacant substance: but the whole of my world hid within me, rather than grow with a boy's excitement incrementally out.

All the neighborhood was ablaze with fragile skeletons, rotting jack-o-lanterns, witches with broomsticks of dimly hinted erotic purpose: all allowed to approach only the houses with porch lights set generously on. No dark mysteries. No chance for razor blades or rat poison. No vermillion seas of the hallucinogenic. No invitations inside to see the sincerest of decorations; to sample the orderly, though wicked, punch; to select the best of the treats that lead to a comforting lap.

I could see every detail of this, but my costume kept me from any complementary participation. I sprang onto the porches like a large mouthed bass out of the lake my elder brothers and their dates parked along to learn sex: and no one saw me. I held out my sack, as rumpled as yesterday's underwear, and no one dropped anything in. I made the most terrifying of the horrible faces I knew how to make. No one shuddered. My costume was flawless, and I but an atom in the great construction of this magic evening.

People looked through me as though I were the window glass of a small town shopping district. Their focus was always on the sales tag behind, the extent of the mark down. I could feel their breathing when they leaned over me to service the goblins and ghosts sequenced at my back. I shouted the names of people I recognized; I reached up, as though I were the troll beneath their garden bridges, as their hands passed by with the treats I craved: yet always those hands blessed some other monster.

I was the last child to go home. I put away my empty sack. I took off my costume and folded it into the box where I keep it now, still stored within reach. I began to prepare myself with no ambling regrets for my evening bath.

My mother stopped by the door to my room, her corn silk hair wrapped around her dizzying neck and spreading across her over-pressed shoulders like envy. Skillfully she asked "Why, there you are! Where have you been so long?"

And I, breaking the engineered imagination of my face, said, "Here, all the time: I have been no more, no less, than here." And the voices of the limitless thousands I had been that night, and would be every night forever more, began to stagger out of me like the spring's melt water, like the last of our spilt milk, like something I was always supposed to guiltlessly know but up to now could only mutter unintelligibly through. I was the everyone and the no one she feared I might one grieving day be.

TRADING CRAFTS

Our artisans have been crafting wooden statues for as long as we have had access to wood. Formerly, they would sit all day in the dirt outside of their indefensible houses, scraping for centuries with stone, and then later with knives. Everyone in the village would take a figurine and leave a week's cornmeal or a side of beef. To have a figurine was to be a paying part of the village: reliable, accountable.

In the more recent years the artisans have set up tables and chairs, have pocket knives that fold into hard handles, have wood stacked in their sturdier houses ready for use. The tourists have done this to them. With hard currency, value has gotten out of kilter. What to us was once enough to keep a man and his thinning family alive for a week is now three or four pieces of paper, themselves then exchanged for provisions and the labor of another man to keep the roof together and the walls plastered.

Each man will sit in his chair, leaning his elbows on the table, often smoking one of the cigarettes the government exchange officers will leave as payment in kind for a go with one of the village free girls; and which the carvers get in exchange for a wooden carving of a snarling turtle, or a mime-toothed comb shaped like the face of an owl. The carvers will shave away larger pieces of wood than they would have discarded in the past, proving to themselves how deeply their art lies in the natural world, how much human effort it takes to get it out. Waste is always proof of plenty. As long as the tourist mill pointedly about, the artisans will carve. And they will carve anything.

Of late, the fancy has been especially large animals, or especially frightful ones. Or fertility symbols: renditions of reedy women with huge breasts that, if arrayed on a real woman, a man could curl his whole body around. These are what the tourists understand: busts of women, with nipples that shoot out like an invitation to hunt. Wooden imitations of natively naked women, with the curve of bottomless production in their bellies. Shuffling along in their traveling clothes, visitors will spill out paper and flat metal pieces, and those artisans who can count, count, and argue, and point to the tourist's hand with the most paper, seeking more whether they need more or not, or whether the work of a morning is worth more or not.

It is our belief that the big animals will not make it through the rift between orders of lives. Only the small will manage to crawl to the next plane. In our houses, we have carvings of spiders and frogs and turtles and marmosets. And we have practical fertility charms of both the man and the woman. Some of these are ugly: women with small breasts, where a man would have to squeeze both together to get a stiffening handful; and men whose prongs are high and cautious, and whose testicles could not contain the sputtering serum to cure any woman's fever. But this is what we know there is within all of us, and this is what there will be to work with when worlds change and our village unconsciously renews.

You would not know that, from what our artisans craft these days. Their art looks out, not ahead. A thousand indecent women, only a handful of spear pronged men, and not a blanket to provide imagination for any. The artisans' own clothes are getting better with the ability to trade at outside commercial markets, using sloshing boxes of tourist currency; and from their art's marketability to the world, what they carve looks less like us, less like the world that sings sympathy to us all day, and more like the most extreme of us with tourist faces.

But then the quietly expected event comes to pass: one of our girls gives birth to a child with an extreme of body, parts out of our proportion, fit only for a modern artisan's model, and the face of a tourist. The girl does not deny the act that all know produced the child, thick with the smell of tourist sweat and static electricity. She nurses the half alien thing at a breast that some local man should have blessed with a nearly flat palm during a more natural conception. She embraces the resounding intricacy of the stain that she has no husband. She expects to be the first of many.

From then on we ask: what did the carvers know, and what vengeful visions had they spit at us without our knowing? Were they singing guilelessly our best interests all along? Or are they both blameless and unknowing, mere artisans, and their art no more than what we see in wood that has been disenchanted?

The sound of the monster child's crying can be heard across half the village, rattling with a rhythm that seems to settle in the round corners of our history. Some say it is a laugh. Some say it is the dreary music of want without wanting. All say it is not a sound of community. I say it is nothing but the sound of *more*. And *more* is going to have its way with us all.

THE RIVALS

There was a long line of us there to burn our old shadows. One huge flame, and all of us single file trailing out for as far as anyone could see. At least in the dark. Since each individual seemed to want to stand in front of the flame once he or she had tossed her or his shadow in — watching it bubble and fill with holes and curl furiously up before shifting into a sour smoke and winging away so small it could not disturb even the late night star excesses – the line barely shuffled, seeming to simply shake itself and edge but a foot or two closer.

I am sure those at the back of the line knew only a rumor of fire. They could see perhaps ten, maybe fifteen bodies ahead, and without a spot of light, could only believe that soon they would shuffle near enough that they would imagine a point. Soon they would come close enough to actually see a point. Hours later, that point might begin to shimmy, to act like a flame. Hours and hours and hours away they might see differing heats in the flame, reflected as differing colors, and a dance of heat up and down the slide of the flame. And they would shift their unattached shadow hand to hand in anticipation of eventually feeling the flame's warmth, of hearing the sizzle and imaging the steam of shadows, even though the shadows popped more than sizzled, and produced no steam at all.

Another shadow gone and the one who surrendered it – in this case, a man, a thick set unimpressive man, perhaps of the middle class and surely having much better things to do, with a hat set properly and his jacket off-the-rack but fitting very well, indeed – stepping first in short chops away from the light, then his stride growing as he goes gray in the closing dark, then loping. We would all think of him running, running in the dark, each half pace more joy in his gravity than in the last half pace, and the whole of him shadowless and the man that he remained beginning to breathe as awkwardly and as simply as a running man breathes.

Forgive me, but it was I who first suggested we might use two fires. There were so many of us, I assumed. I could not see the end of the line. But I could feel it pressing on me. I could feel my own desperation at the length of the wait: and I could see the fire! I could see the shadows quivering their last; I was near the point of tossing mine in. Another fire. It was only a suggestion, an idea that might help my saddled and summarized fellow citizens. That doleful and inaccurate long line wearied me. So many of my station and belief, so many of my purpose and collection, so many seemingly stretched endlessly, waiting endlessly, eager endlessly, to complete this one task.

A second fire would enrich the pace. A second fire would expand our success. The fact had nothing to do with me: it was physics, chemistry, geometry, the unburdened science that makes for a world. It was not my fault.

I immediately had allies. The thought was so crisp and untroubled that it clattered decoratively in the wind and was near sex with announcing the utility of itself. The woman behind me placed a hand seductively on my shoulder and said, "What a prickly, marvelous idea!" The nails of her soft fingers were painted an enamel-red that seemed to have no whirls or streaks, but looked as though a natural part of her thrilling anatomy. But the man ahead turned about to face me fully and put a seditious palm to my chest, saying "Wait a moment. We have almost made it. I can taste the fire; my shadow is curing from the heat of the nearby flame. It will not be long for us now."

I marveled at his short sightedness.

I was prepared to note that I meant no offense, but that the mathematics would be compelling: yet, before I could screw my teeth into place, a man slightly back actually stepped out of line to look - it seemed at the time - for kindling, and the line gratefully closed the space he had left. Now a second line was imperative, for there was no way for the man to get back into the one line. He stopped, his shadow listlessly draped over one arm, staring back at the place where he had been, apparently recognizing the person whose back he had for so long been following. Or thinking he recognized it, for it did not matter: he could have been looking at any smoke of a gap, for he was not getting back into the line. There was no opening and his only option would be to go to the end – an end that was but a rumor and might be forever away and in any direction as long as it was the direction away from this end.

Another shadow boiled and rose in pockets of gas and stretched itself on the fire momentarily, then drifted in diaphanous duty into the air, and the rest of us shuffled a half step forward: everyone, absolutely everyone, even those who knew only the rumor of the fire, inched closer to the fire. All of us, except for the man who had stepped out of line.

I was sure the woman who had lauded my idea, the woman with the punctuation of her reddened fingernails, would emerge from the line to join the man; but she slid up behind me, her shoes barely leaving the ground as she glided, her fiercely enameled fingers back at her side, as silent as the distance of contrary planets. I could feel the hope within her. Hope. All that hope and nothing to do with it. Hope like ballast left when cargo replaces it for the journey home.

The man was but ten feet out of line, and all of us close enough to the flame could see that he was more than simply a blur of limbs and features. Someone one day might recognize him. There was enough light leaking from the fire to transfix him. Someone might make a mental note of him and store some special feature, some identifying mark — just as someone who had heard me might yet be storing a snippet of my voice. Many might be thinking that, again - on a subway, or at the back of a restaurant, or mounting a fire engine – they might catch a flog of this voice and know what meaning it once had been filled with, how full and finely laced it was, and how many brother echoes it ensured.

I could not for the stuffing within me look long at him. He was but a point of distance.

The man then reached into his pocket and brought out a simple cigarette lighter. One of those not meant to be refilled, but which, once gone lame, is tossed into the ashbin and forgotten. I think it had a light green case, for I could see it reflected in the flame. He held it initially in thumb and forefinger, his elbow yet bent, with eyes that I could not see probably regarding the artifact, eyes perhaps already tearful with his intent.

Another shadow was successfully consumed, and we moved forward. The sound of shuffling shimmied down the line, to eventually die out far back in the fallow dark. I could feel the heat now, and I knew I was less than a cohort removed from the flame. In but a while, the man and his lighter would be well behind me, and turning back to view him too uncomfortable to do often enough to keep his narrative alive.

When the man rolled the metal ignition cylinder and an elfin spark growled, we all took in the breath we did not know we were holding. We had been autonomically holding it since the lighter was first brought out, our thoughts racing ahead action to action to action to result to mitigation. Flame! Flame!

He dropped his shadow to the ground and raised the small flame. It was similar to the larger one we were moving to, but nearly free of soot and the ashes of shadow, and we turned to see him: the man out of line with the flame over his head. The shadow lay bunched at his feet and the flame flickered flickered flickered, flickering at arm's length.

He could have put the two together.

A woman, blessedly simple and focused, stepped suddenly out of line; a small heap of a woman who must have been drilled in duty; a woman knowing I suppose what needed to be done. She folded her shadow over her shoulder as the line cleverly closed in, eliminating the pearly blankness she had left. Wisely bent like an expression of grief, she began with her dim and unkempt fingers to rummage around mutely within the dark left at ground. Thankfully, it seemed she was looking for kindling. It was all I think she could do. I am sure she is doing it still.

Others will join her. I know they will. And every blinding inch of it will be my fault.

There is a half-step forward, the line shrugging and the noise of its dragging feet hurled off into the challenging dark, changing its timbre as it slips unbidden away from the heat and the light and the consummation of mission: sidling crab-like away into the recesses of hope and the salting saliva of doing what can be done. Away. Away.

THE AGITATION

When I think there are enough washing machines, someone drives up in a red ramshackle truck, one fender barely hanging on, the rush of a circus clown in the lion's pen, and pushes off yet another washing machine. That would be someone who thinks there are not enough. I can take his word for it.

I am waiting for there to be a quorum. But I do not know how many washing machines make for a quorum. I would think this many would be enough, but I do not know everything. Obviously, the man now driving with a lightened truck quickly away believed we were at least one short. But he may have other motives. Perhaps his washing machine had simply just worn out.

Most likely, the washing machines themselves will decide when a quorum has been reached, when there are enough in attendance to make decisions that the remaining washing machines will honor. They will appoint one of the less dented machines and that machine will draw itself up into a mounted version of a manufacturer's ideal showroom model and report: there is a quorum. But for now, they have divided themselves into front loaders and top loaders and sit in their own frowning and white-paneled subjective like-member caucuses. Before a congress with a quorum can decide, it has to be decided what comprises a quorum.

But I do not think they are debating what comprises a quorum. I do not hear the clothes baskets clanging, nor the spin cycle compromising. I do not see the lids flapping nor hear the hose attachments hissing. Each caucus has its back to the other, and the only thing that stops the unanimously querulous, grinding washing machine doors is the arrival of a new, previously unobserved machine: will it top load or front load?

I think about the quorum. Can I determine what number makes a quorum with my own independent mathematics: deduce the number out of my own effort, without the opinion of the assembled washing machines? Or is the number of the quorum not a point of decision but an established and known fact that I do not know. Or is it an agreement? Is it waiting to be handed defiantly to me, like the unchanging truth of mechanical lizard hearts: matter-of-factly on a folded piece of stock paper, by one washing machine that sticks out its water softener tray casually and provides to me - a presence less than mechanical - my education on quorum numbers while on the edges of its paneling it is backing away?

The washing machines' metal shimmers of dry desert heat and I stand farther back. Red ones, black ones, white ones, beige ones: all huddle in their inward facing circular caucuses, presumably considering all the things that will be settled when the pedantically awaited quorum is reached. Great things can be done. Issues put to bed. Process concluded. Dishwashers detained.

I have faith.

But my faith may be only that the necessary number will be reached, not that, once achieved, the quorum which will have then a command of the possible, will be able to prod its potential into progress. Dolt that I can be, sometimes I think too much of opportunity and not enough of the use of that opportunity. The desires and thoughts of a washing machine are beyond me, and I do not know how disenchanting the needs of any one machine or caucus of machines might be. I put my faith in the number in order to achieve it; but, achieving it, am I then nothing more than one step closer to preparing to set another goal?

The washing machines tilt forward their lids, or open askew their front doors, each nodding to each in a respect that does not extend much below the soft metal that houses their more eclectic machinery. I am to them invisible.

Another lilting truck pulls up, but there is no washing machine teetering in the back, no recently un-hosed and hoisted cleaning service unit sitting in the truck bed. Out from the flaked onion-paint driver's side, a woman of no light, no charm, and with nothing to recommend her to even the most celibate of memories, steps ungainly, but steadily, away from the barely quivering four wheeled conveyance. She walks in the shortest of unprincipled steps to the squat passenger side door, squarely opens that brooding door, and takes out, with a brazen bend and a bottom braced jolt, a heroically yellow and overflowing basket of laundry. She turns to look sensuously at all the stunned washing machines. Her hair flips in the wind just as it would in better writers' stories, and she looks down the length of her seemingly once broken nose, sweeping her head side to side in survey. Anyone can see her breath willfully burdening the air around her.

Why yes, she has a reason to be here.

THE GROWING COMPROMISE

Like most, I thought the Spinners a fad. Something that had come out of nowhere, established itself like crabgrass or dandelion paupers in the shrubbery. Perhaps they were the victims of the ill-adopted custom of another country. Foppery.

We thought the adherents could not keep up the constant twirling, could not find ways to fit the necessaries of their lives into the spinning style. So many practical things could not be done while spinning. Balance just in spinning was trouble enough. How could they sew or harvest or sweep or climb ladders with a spin? Surely, they would soon start a list of exceptions, and it would grow until spinning itself was the exception vice the rule, and eventually common sense would lead them back to common sense.

We Straight-walkers were suspicious of their perversely sidling ways.

But then, there were small businesses that began to cater to them. Instruments with customized handles, differently angled faces, platforms vice steps, were created. Industry rushes in to meet the opportunities of even insanity. Spinners became a source of revenue for many. So many new accoutrements had to be created, a reasonable slice of market could be made out of servicing the silliness of Spinners. We laughed as we watched them learn new ways to open doors, engage crosswalk signals, accomplish a meal, collect groceries. When a new-fashioned tool could assist them, an entrepreneur would step in, find a solution, make a profit, make it easier to be a Spinner.

A level of acceptance, along economic opportunity, was afforded them. But they were still an expression of ill-fitting.

I laughed with all the others until I saw Mirabo spin by. We had had some exchanges when we were both Straight-walkers; but now, Mirabo as a Spinner had more presence twirling with her, an extra weight. Her face spinning past seemed to flash of new purpose; her lilt was more erect, more confident even in this bizarre practice. Physically, as with all the Spinners, she was thinner than common for our society, ceding calories to the spin, growing leaner and more longly muscular. But she had added somehow to her cadence, expanded her grasp of the metaphysical, seized a gravity she had not possessed before. When at first she spun by, I was amused – but then my eyes were inclined to follow her, to notice how elegant her spinning was, if you let go of its impracticality. She seemed to pull a bit of primordial, exciting space with her.

Our first date was a negotiation of norms. The rhythm of her speech conformed to the twirling of her head: pauses held until she was speaking away from me, content saved for when her mouth was rotating pleasantly back towards me. All of that date was an exploration of how a Straight-walker might have a more than casual relationship with a Spinner. We could not be careful. We could not afford to think our focus forward: the smothering practicalities of even our tentative togetherness required us to see a relationship as being conquered or consolidated by the physics required to make the relationship hold competing and cooperating dimensions.

What we learned is that to be a couple, each must give up something. The Straight-walker must understand the centripetal force of the Spinner; the Spinner must understand the fixed gravity that lurks everywhere around and which is the sustenance of the Straight-walker. One is an imposition, one is a choice, though which is which changes.

As the relationship moved on, we learned that many of the most cherished intimacies can only be accomplished when couples spin together – which, paradoxically is one partner spinning, and the other stationary, affixed to the one spinning. Odd that the pinnacle of spinning could be a matter of being fixed, tethered to someone else who is spinning, spinning one's self only at the impetus of the partner. But there is canon for it.

When we announced our marriage, both sets of parents were disapproving. Mixed marriages at the time were unheard of. Everyone wondered how any intimacy could be accomplished, not only Straight-walker to Spinner, but even Spinner to Spinner. The canon was in its infancy. The physics and biomechanics were our experiments. Our reports to the field were the map of future tolerances. It was difficult to speak of, but we spoke.

Our families were despairing of children. How could we produce? Greater than their horror at the likelihood of our barrenness was their horror of imagination at how we might produce, the Straight-walker and the Spinner. The mechanics of it was what befuddled and angered them.

But when Mirabo at last conceived, their consuming worry was: Straight-walker or Spinner? I tried to advise all sides that neither of us knew, that it was not within our power to decide. We would be as surprised as they, as much in the dark, as consumed with the mathematics of expectations as they.

As the time for Mirabo's confinement approaches, we fill the room our spinning mid-wife has suggested for the birth with pillows, foam, and volumes of the soft. Mirabo will spin at the center, creating her own gravity, arms out or in as the contractions demand. I will be kept in the room one over until the event has passed, pacing in my straight lines, subject to gravity but not creating it. Only when all is concluded will I be told: the new life looks but one way at a time and howls a consistent birth-moan — or around and around and around goes the hybrid's attention, the cries rising and falling and rising circularly in tonal frequency. I am sure I will love my child in lines or circles as best fits the geometry of needs.

THE KINDLY CORRECTION

"Hey, I want some chickens!" Thus began the yearning for empire in the methodically mendacious mind of Farmer One.

"But you are a cattle farmer: you have no need for chickens." Farmer Two was less likely to see an upset to the current order of events as bringing profit to anyone. His poultry farm was beginning to do better than his books could hide.

"But chickens right now are trading, production cost to market, twelve percent higher than cattle!" Farmer One, with his lock on the mathematics of the moment, had a point.

"But cattle are a longer-term investment, and you can hold them until the market turns." It is true: cattle have a longer shelf life as sentient stock than chickens.

"So, would you like some cattle?"

And so the great exchange was made. Farmer One, who had grasslands planned around fences, and water broken from the neighbors' stream, and feeding troughs that worked almost semi-autonomously like meticulous orgasm producing machines, got a thousand chickens from Farmer Two. Farmer Two, whose coops stretched behind his house like stray but allied locusts, and whose pens were the epitome of mannered disagreement, received a thousand head of cattle from Farmer One.

Economic diversity is the soul of nationhood, the basis of solid citizenry, the parent of profit: the heat-wave diva with her skirt hitched up and a thumb pushed out on the desolate path of highway you happen to be, with moral ambiguity and fresh hand cuffs, driving with no anticipations along.

Within the week the chickens were pulling less diligently at Farmer One's grass than they would need to if they were to survive. They were not fully cooperating with the sudden shift from chicken feed to grazing pasture. And some had already fallen into the open water and discontentedly drowned. To Farmer One's surprise, his cattle had avoided the poultry and overgrazed on just one vellum-thin spit of pasture, and were themselves growing as thin as the children in those disregarded pictures of poverty one finds in the natural science magazines that Farmer One would secretly enjoy with his bourbon slug just before bed. He could see through the haze of earlier expectations that this season would be insurance and price supports and the sound of chickens dying before securing him profit.

Within the week, Farmer Two was lamenting the condition of his coops. Not as sturdy as he thought, the wooden sides had been shattered by cattle unwilling to yield to the chicken feed, cattle ramming through the structures like stranded baleen whales nonetheless intent on ravishing krill. The wire pens curled over on themselves in godless surrender and multitudes of chickens were crushed in the disloyal metal wire lying down. Cattle sang all night of the hunger that clung about them like the speed of amusement park roller coasters, keeping Farmer Two and his wife in bed awake and as taut as glass kitchen knives. Farmer Two could imagine this season would be the bodies of intemperate cattle, unclaimed feathers, a disaster grant, price supports, and a summer employment program the insurance consortium would recommend.

All through the valley shop owners and day laborers and laundry merchants sighed, rolled over heavily in sagging beds, and committed a blind, angry sex ineptly at the frustration in their lives. All this ending season they would be holding rare income closely, with each knock on the door bringing the blue satin likelihood of the insurance man: his shoulders as broad as starving rain barrels; one hand balled into a mathematical fist, the other open with spent desire and the yellow of enveloping displeasure. The once reasonable premium levied during good times would be awash in his palm, his face frowning forward, and his oracular mouth demanding more, demanding surcharge, demanding a restoration of profitability.

Every merchant would lean back into that face of need and shout "Pay the two farmers first. We need their business, we need their disposable income. Make good their losses, and then we can pay more!" And the insurance collectors would think grandly intricate thoughts, sliding their premiums ever larger until the premiums were a velvet noose about the public's neck. The insurance collectors have always known that the insurance company does not have the money, it is merely a conduit. The insurance men would imagine, with imaginations as broad as the backside of the ocean, that the public might look to be on toe-tip at the edge of their imaginative bench, alive with the invigoration of their insurance payment nooses, and that there is only more business to be gathered by teasing them to step credulously off, suspended by their uninsured necks in nothing but common air. Common air, being sold by people who do not own it, to people who will not need it, for the good of people who will waste it, by the mouthful.

And the two farmers meet at the tavern and explain to one another that it is the insurance that allows them to innovate, to secure themselves against mistake, and to make new products for the masses. Products the public will pay dearly for, after they pay their insurance.

Across the street, a day-jobber offers minimum wage to anyone who will bury chickens, bury cows, repair fences.

THE CREATION OF WEALTH

I make a living fashioning spears. I have my shop at the back of my house, stack my raw materials in a shed just beyond the outhouse. The shavings and stone flakes left of my industry go into the garden. Every part of the production chain is accounted for, and my efforts are to the public good.

The overall design of my spears was originally very basic. I could deliver varying lengths of shaft, differing angles to the spear head, lash the stone to wood with better leather or more of it in the more expensive models. But what I added, to what might have remained a common sense stick with a point, was merely the persistence of stone at the business end, and an eye to balance the added weight against length. When tossed, my spears do not tumble. They do not shimmy like reeds in the wind. When they strike the point does not break off, nor does it thump ineffectively dull against hide. I earn my premiums.

I would not be a spearmaker if I did not have a good eye for business. This is no religion; it is art only so long as it keeps the artist fed. I noted early in crafting my business model that some people would buy more than one spear. Some would buy back up spears, and some auxiliary spears. Some would buy entire families of spears, two or three at a time, and then store them at home in every room, eerily ready for the hunt or for battle, prepared from any exit route across the topology of their living spaces. Volume matters. I cannot grow so fond of the beauty of one spear that I lose track of the utility of the many spears.

At first, I merely experimented with different spearheads. I could make them narrow and knife like, or I could flatten them out like a hammer with a point. Once I had given up the practical, I could fathom spearheads of innumerable clans, many seeming to have no possible purpose, no use in any endeavor native to my customers. It was never my intent to justify or fulfill need, but rather to simply sell spears. It is the regular geometry of cash in hand that in the end is my motivation.

Some of these new spears suffered a loss of balance, and in the air were triumphantly in-artful and clumsy, rounding out the trip from throw to ground like a wounded bird filtering the feather drift for lift and finding none. Not only does this not matter, but it seems the smaller the potential uses for my wares, the more prized they are. I command a higher price for items that can have no worth except in their possession alone.

I have begun to add feathers and other adornments. At first, I would not add beads because they would interfere with the murderous function of my exquisite killing devices, but I have learned that such does not matter. Those who spend the most on my creations often have the least ability to consummate a fatal action. The opulence of their spears compensates for the lack of lethality in their abilities. So I now have adorning shreds of waste metal and additional baubles strung with strips of leather or surplus cloth, entwined beneath the head or along the shaft, flowing so far behind the main business article that they drag on the ground behind the owner as he carries his spear explosively in the street, strutting so as to make the trail behind him a barrier to those who inattentively follow.

I am working on a spear that it would take three men to hurl. It would not go far, and would most likely land without inflicting any damage, but it will be unique and unquestioned. Surely it will be bought by a man who has no intention to arrange any collection of his neighbors so that he and they can toss it. It will sit in his living room, extending out one of his windows and become in the dark an impediment to clear passage. He will recline satisfied in one corner of his receiving room and consider it as though it were a trophy, as though it were the head of some fearsome beast he had himself felled, or the ears of a dozen maimed enemies. It will be placed in his boasting chants as through it could be used to defend his honor, or make revenge for the childhood slights of his past which now so violently drive his present needs.

There is no extreme I cannot sell. The fact of the spear itself supersedes the use of the spear. Each bedazzling armament creates the market for the next constructed escalation. I have an industry that feeds itself its own ever-growing output as its next regenerating input: a feedback loop that means I will forever have business.

You should consider the depth and breadth of your own arsenal. Has it become out of date? Is it too small for your place in the hierarchy? Have you felt too often that being civilized is your only option? Surely, you remember that time, long ago, though seeming sweetly like this last weary Tuesday, when you were pushed from behind by one of the older boys; and he and his leathery mates would not let you up, knocking you back and placing a conquering knee to your chest, laughing. How you squirmed and the other children transfixedly watched you, some in pity, some in delight, and all you could think of was how you might escape, then how you might avenge: how to pound the even out of the odd.

I am always building the next. While the intent of my devices may be small, the show I can make them put on is as large as the thunder of an unseen storm. You can reaffirm your soul; you can create a balance in the randomly arranged history of your grievances. Purchase, perhaps, a magnificent spear that you cannot lift with one hand, that has to be balanced across one struggling shoulder or the other, and, if allowed to sway too far one way or another, cannot by anyone be controlled.

Go ahead. I dare you.

COMFORT

"For once, I wish you would not insist on carrying your dead cats back to Connecticut for burial."

She stared off into space, holding the suitcase with both hands, her grief being controlled by the mechanics of her mission. With method, emotion can be mathematics, and so can be solved into a manageable equation.

"If they knew you had a dead cat in the suitcase, they would not let you board."

I was immaterial to the proceedings. When we lived in Connecticut, I could indulge the depth of her sorrows. I even had a part in the rituals of her grief. We had cats. Many cats. Some would die. She would make of each a custom burial. I would be given my part in the grand play she was conducting and I would gladly fulfill my cameo role. I kept waiting for the whole affair to grow greater than us – to grow into something she wanted to make part of the community, or to at least populate with an amen corner of those she felt in tune with her otiose honors for the deceased cats.

But we moved from Connecticut. Pulled ourselves up like weeds with better opportunity and moved from the land of our beginning to the land of rush and ruin. Here, in New York, I wondered if she would recreate her rituals, find a new vacant spot of land, consecrate some new area outside of human traffic, and, as our short-lived cats expired, commit them to this new slit of suddenly sacred ground.

And then Mr. Norman died. He had grown far too obese, and, at 23 or so pounds, was a coronary waiting to happen. He was stiff one morning under the kitchen table, folded in on himself as though he were trying to hide in the vacuum between air molecules, and I thought

– what now? Do we go exploring at the darker edges of our neighborhood for a likely bone yard? Do we drive out to the loamy edges of the island? Is there someplace she has picked out and kept in mind for just such an emergency?

No. She bought a train ticket. Only one train ticket. And she took an old, forties style suitcase, packed it with deodorizer, towels, and Mr. Norman, and called a cab. Even though she had only a train ticket for herself – none for me – nonetheless I accompanied her in the cab. Half silently, only — as I was talking the whole time, and she said nothing. I am sure the cab driver thought we were crazy. We were crazy.

Myself, I would send the pet to a crematorium. But I found myself arguing for sacred spots in New York, and arguing there was nothing special in Connecticut. And there was no argument in return: she was taking Mr. Norman to Connecticut.

That was four trips ago. Four fellow mammals felled. I have made all the arguments I can make. I have offered all the defenses I can muster. I have found amazing potential burial spots – spots with history, spots with beauty, spots with a cachet of honor. Spots that seemed to call out, needing a reason to be special, capable of shouldering responsibility. She is unmovable.

And yet, in the throes of her unbearable mathematics, she is the most intricate thing I have ever seen. And, in a way, I wish when it is my time to be released, that I might fit reasonably in a suitcase. A trunk, perhaps a suit bag – with my towels and my deodorizer, pleasantly curled into the form of the conveyance, myself looking forward to the trip. It might be worth the devotion.

Despite there being a better side to a failure, I wickedly hope that during the wriggling, dolorous train ride, no one suspects the cat in the luggage. I could never rebalance her.

THE LIBERATOR

I seek the hoarders of light. I follow their excess radiance, canvas their illuminated neighborhoods. Where I have suspicions I check their gaudy cars for hidden compartments, query their relatives, look for patterns in their spiral friendships. I research unexplained wealth, suddenly revealed balloon payments: match the timing of their good fortunes with an infusion of light onto the easily triggered, endlessly adjusting, black markets. I look for a cockiness that belies the hoarder's otherwise usual and threadbare social station.

Anyone can be a hoarder. I have caught children as young as seven, and old men as wrinkled and outside of their skin as conglobulated waste paper. They leave a little excess light in their pants pockets, or fill a back bedroom with more than the tinseling windows can stand. It does not matter why, or how wonderful. It does not matter the sanctions of joy it brings. It violates the law.

Most have no clue concerning the intricacies they are slack-handedly dealing with. It starts with lingering sunlight strangled out of an unwatched window, and soon moves on to muttered scrapping from an emergency flashlight. Tatters of light become tangles of rays become buckets of radiance. In the end it will be a house full of common lamps, light laid out everywhere: in all the drawers and all the cabinets; and the dark, with its victim's heart torn out, bursting out from the shadowed front door to make its own crestfallen accusations.

To afford more glass and mirror space to store their collected light, they will start off by selling a little of their older, more clumsily secured light: and that is when I have a trail to follow. I let the individual buyers go, their thimbles of light certainly illicit still, but nothing compared to a real hoarder's boxes and cloven racks of tethered photons. I want to access the knowledge of those who have learned to harvest light, to preserve irradiation, to keep it shining for their own all-consuming selfish pleasures: the marshalling of light loose in their own tight, exotically shut places.

I am the line against which there is only so much day and night, so much energy generation and so much dissolution. I put on my black hat and black coat and wriggle into the night with my quiver of weightless crime leads. I know there will never be enough light for all, and that all light must be fairly rationed. No one has a right to hold more than his or her ephemeral share. Our illuminated society thrives on getting and giving, not on keeping.

I have no idea why some otherwise ordinary citizens are driven to hoard. Their object is not profit. Their pride is only personal. If I do not catch them, eventually the light itself pushes them out of their brittle homes and one day explodes into a fanfare of brilliance running, simply and uncritically, in every direction: away. At the beginning there is the passion of possession, with an erotic tinge in sympathetically accomplishing the profane. But it does not last. The obsession grips them like an incubus in an elegant nightmare of dusk and their lives become ever more the stealing and stacking, the inventory and preservation, the frenzy of more and more and ever more. In every hoarder I catch there is a crescent of moral relief at the climax of their apprehension: a falling away of their obtuse, by then almost parenthetical need.

In the end, they try to ruin the physics. The light itself turns against them and they secede from magic and join common science in trying to maintain control. Given long enough, their alchemy can braze buildings, eviscerate entire neighborhoods. They work in their goggles and lead lined aprons, praying there is a way to tame the light they have so lovingly gathered: the light that broke first out of the box, then out of the closet, then out of the room, and now threatens the house.

But I get most of them long before it unhinges to that. I see small signs. I look to the singe of unlikely skin; follow the bends of gravity around otherwise unimposing structures; find dark that looks so ordinary and commonplace that it must be an imposter.

Oh, you should see their faces when I set the hoarded light free! Their mouths drop open and expose the great blackness within, the dim cold of their unfired internals, as the once hoarded light disentangles and in a flash goes back to meet the external dark it was always conjoined with. The tears come out of the accused like a purring acid rain and all they have left are the finger burns gained from fondling their fleeting, but once transiently captured, brilliance.

I stare into their shadowing eyes and imagine that they have learned their lessons, and now are ready to be ordained in the currency of an ordinary physics; but I always see, in their growing ethics of refractory crystallization, that they have not the skill to reform. They will, one day, drag their fingers across some stray mirror, and again be stung.

CONSEQUENCES

There are so many of them, each without the grace of even looking wounded. I gather them in the folds of my apron, not unmindful that, were I to clasp them too tightly, the yellow skin might dimple, or reverently pop completely in. And while, for some, the skin would pop back, for many the crease would remain.

Oh, I remember now, it does not matter. We are to do with them as we will, either way.

Not more than fifty yards away, the struggle still rages. My children at waterside reach as far as they dare to snare yellow duck after yellow duck from the mass that is working to go past this point. As the children make a hole where once a duck unwisely floated, another duck fills in – and so the mass by mutual gravity and the tension of free water is pulled shoreward.

All of these ducks were released not more than half an hour ago, dropped individually into our river by people who paid a dollar to paste them with some private list of wants and then set the burdened ducks loose to dumbly find their way supposedly to the sea. Wishes for fine mates, for a healthy pet, for the recovery of a grandmother, for wealth, for children, for the injury of a transgressor. Wishes, wishes, wishes. The ducks do not care, and dutifully ferry their releasers' scrawled wants idly along the river's dominant stream. Ducks set free.

Free? What good is a plastic duck without confinement? What good does it do anyone? What child names it, what bully smashes it, what parent hides memories in it?

I say it is nothing but plastic trash: trash made in a recognizable shape. You might see it as something resembling the pliant bath mates of your childhood. Do not be fooled. Free, it is only unlikable plastic given a sympathetic shape.

I hold as many as I can in this apron. They would not have made it to the sea, anyway. There are too many squares in the river, too much marshland, too many masters of trash that have been in the water longer and that will not abide trespassers.

My eldest daughter sorts them: ducks that can be resold to the releasers upstream; ducks that should be buried or burned; ducks that might go to the cousins or nephews or the lukewarm friends of bathing relatives. Every so often I keep one for myself, and add the re-enlivened object to my flock on the kitchen window sill. I have them in rows, leaning over-grayed inward, where I can watch them envy the rain outside, beyond the window of my work parlor.

Every so often, saturated from its time in the water, a wish falls from its mooring under a duck. Carefully, without reading it, we pick the spent paper up, pat it out, and paste it back as best we can. The glue would have never held in the ocean, anyway. Once that work is done, then we can continue to process the resupplied duck as though nothing had happened. Placed on my window ledge, or sold again, or given to bath mates, buried or burned. It is really all the same.

COMMUNITY EVOLVED

As the whale enters the intersection, well-meaning beach-goers commandeer children's buckets and scoop water, rushing in to toss the water on the lumbering whale. It is what they have seen on television. The whale continues its undulations, getting in each contraction a few feet farther from the road. People, who would otherwise have no purpose, form a bucket line: multiple sand pails in this process going hand to hand and then onto the whale. As the whale gets farther from the shore, more people join in the hydration line, even people who were not originally at the beach but who came from businesses and off the sidewalk, united in this sudden design, this bizarre civic commitment. The whale cannot speak, cannot communicate, can only ride this labored linear locomotion Those in the bucket line are reveling in their new positions, in their new prestige of public purpose, in their appreciation of their great charity. The whale is evolving. The whale is thinking no more water, no water. The line of potential bucket-minders stretches now past the whale, tries to predict where the whale is likely to go. They want to be ready to be useful. As the whale slips out of true straight, the line shuffles to adjust—those far ahead who cannot see the whale but have only heard of the dilemma reacting to shifting shoulders, the whole of the great line whiplashing, citizens quick to mirror the new projected path. The rumor at the last of the line is that this has something to do with a whale.

THE CURIOUS COMMITMENT

I heard the water running as I first stepped in. I sat down my backpack, letting it slide into its usual place in the spotted green chair just inside the door, and twisted my body fully around to push the door closed, set the thumb lock, and draw the chain. I could see through the evaporating crack nothing behind me in the hall, nothing on the floor outside the door, no obvious pathways to the unordinary. The backpack settling into the chair slipped to the seat cushion's edge and nearly fell.

I should have long ago given up my pretensions and bought a briefcase, but with the backpack I get the practical means to carry all of my papers and my lunch, yet can look still like a hopeful student. I once was a student, and I lived out of my backpack. Today, no one would know I was making a good living: that I have means, and a professional roundness.

I have lived alone for three years. It is a decent apartment. Not too large, not too small. Not too cluttered, not too free of clutter. The walls not needing paint, but not looking just painted. Bric-a-brac not seeming staged, but looking to be perhaps the idle yet collectable flotsam of a life still in the making.

From the pattern of notes, I could tell the water running was obviously in the shower: the shower set anachronistically in a free-standing tub, with feet, and a shower curtain that runs all the way around the tub on a suspended frame. It was one of the draws of the apartment. Most of these apartments have been upgraded with more modern features, but there was room in this one to leave the overwrought bathtub and accommodate it with unique features and conveniences: so this apartment's bathroom looks like no other apartment's bathroom in this wickedly modernized building. The sink has its own pedestal and the toilet cowers in an abbreviated corner. There are toiletry shelves and a clothes hamper and a small closet for linen and supplies, and the smell of tile secure in its history.

All of this I knew from memory, as I was suspended still standing by the door, listening.

With the unevenness of the water, not only was the shower running, but someone, or something, sounded to be actively using that shower. There were catches in the water, and releases where it hit the base of the tub undeterred. It had been years since I had listened closely to the symphony of someone taking a shower. When showering one's self, the sound is different. Contained. When you take your own shower, there is a purpose to everything and every sound has its cause and you pay it no attention. But listen to someone else take a shower, and the noises are explosions of unexpected contentions, sudden reversals and heartening advances, mis-directions and discoveries. Nothing like rain, but more like surgery.

I checked the furniture to make sure it was mine. I remembered the number on the door, and it was mine. I knew the key worked and the latch, which had been set on my arrival, with that key had opened. I could see into the kitchen and the twisted refrigerator had my reminders pasted on it. I was in the right place: the person, or thing, in the shower was not.

Slowly I began to edge down the hall. I did not want to startle anyone, least of all myself. The unknown showering entity could be one of the maintenance men. It could be a neighbor, somehow let in mistakenly. It could be a waiting axe murderer, come in through one of the two windows leased with the apartment. I did not want to bring the situation to a terrifyingly early, or unmanageable, conclusion. I figured anything resembling haste would not be an advantage.

I slipped off my shoes and placed them on the couch. I would be quieter in socks alone. I steadied myself against the wall, fingertips only, my hands bent into spiders of light pressure. Apprehension curled my nails and curiosity fogged my glasses. I would not say I was afraid; more closely, I was stalking this uncharted enigma. Someone or something unknown was in my apartment: and it was taking a shower.

One foot after another, my head held slightly forward, it seemed a textbook eternity passed as I was slithering down the hall. Stepping bare inches at first, and then simply sliding my feet, I was a contortion: stiff and unyielding, yet almost proudly mechanical in my march to the noise. I had never seen my apartment walls in such detail, and I marveled at the surprisingly varied textures I had thought nothing of just the morning before. Here a bubble, here a picture from a family reunion four years ago, here a waxed painting from a downtown art show purchased during the hottest early spring I could remember.

I came eventually to the door frame: painted wood with a series of bevels, rolling fields of woodwork mired in three inches of common ostentation. The door to the bathroom itself hung open. Steam had not yet collected sufficiently in the room to come billowing out into the hallway. Perhaps the water was not hot enough. I placed one hand on the ledge and edged my head slightly forward into the open wonder-fall and into a line of sight with the shower.

The shower curtain was translucent, though not transparent; and its translucence had begun to wear. But had the occupant of my tub been a bear or a bison, I could have seen it for the color and shape in an instant. As it was, I could see a human body, one that rippled in the folds of the curtain, distorting itself with ordinary motion. The light from high on the wall over the vanity played with it in small degrees, but was diffuse enough to defeat shadows. As the body moved I could tell through bite sized portions that it was small, female, perhaps of age in the twenties or maybe thirties or possibly forty. A little longer in observation I could tell she had dark hair, and had wetted it and it hung down her back past the clavicle, even while still free to slide around her back and play games with the muscles diving unconcerned into her waist line.

I did not recognize her. She was not one of the neighbors that I knew, though I did not know all of my neighbors. As she dipped and faced the shower then faced away, ever more features became available and the picture I was building of her grew more accurate each sweetening second. I was becoming confident of all the people she could not be. At what is preciously now some elastic point, I was almost certain I had never seen her, that I had no substantive connection to her; and that her presence in my shower was some cosmic calamity that had nothing whatsoever to do with me, other than location and time and perhaps curious opportunity.

She rubbed the top of her left shoulder with her right hand and then pulled at her neck. Her hair billowed, but lay flat against the rough side of her hand, streaming water down her back and in a river bed pattern onto the top of her leg before losing the arc and falling free.

I could not know why the sound of someone else taking a shower is so distinct, is so different from one's own utilitarian sound. I think it is like rain on the remains of a distant camp fire where unhappy men have gathered to rid their lands of monsters. I do not pretend to know the source of the fascination, or the depth of the organics that create the difference. It was my water, my tub, and I did not recognize its voice, nor the weathered music it was happily making.

I do not know why.

The physics of water in a controlled stream surrendered unbound to gravity is the same for each of us, even if we perceive it differently. It is all the same. What I might believe in it is a private matter. But its singularity unites us. It is owned by all of us in common.

I had to come to the conclusion. The only conclusion that could come of this serendipitously strange commonplace. I began ever so cautiously to unbutton my pleasantly secure shirt. Here, in my breached home, still I could use the slither of a shower.

MIGRATION'S END

In past years, someone would come in to announce at the Temperance Bar and Grill or the Post Office or yell across from the set of pumps next at the gas station, "The holes are coming in early this year – just saw one at ….." The fence outside of Johnson's soybean field, or beside the steps to the library, or on the sidewalk just outside the laundromat. Every year the holes are early, though they always start coming in at about the same time each year, as making the arrival early adds a bit of excitement to an otherwise bland statement of fact. "Early" makes the announcer more observant, the event smelling a little special.

Every year the holes come in, first in the farms and abandoned industrial sites strewn around the boundaries of our town. A hole shows up in a dirt road used by farmers to move farm equipment between fields. A hole settles just beyond where a working barn door swings. A woman living just at the edge finds a new hole down the center of her not-quite-long-enough clothesline as she stumbles about in the too high grass with too many wet clothes and not enough clothespins.

Later, holes start showing up in paved roads, or little depressions creep into front yards. One year a sinkhole large enough to swallow the fountain over at city hall moved in and swallowed the fountain over at city hall. By the end of any hole season, everyone is moving about town with their heads down, watching for holes, old and new. Long term residents just adapt to it; newbies trip and scan side to side, step gingerly and ask long time locals how long does this last, how long before the holes move on?

Given a few months of holes, and everyone getting a bit frayed - even if they are too stoic to admit it - the things begin their migration back or on: away. Season's end, and the holes start to leave. First a few, just like when they arrived; then more, ever more in small flocks and occasionally a great extended murder of holes. Off they go and the burdened roads heal, the gleeful trip hazards just at the edge of porch stoops dry up and the home's occupants quiver in relief – gone is something they have had to look for to miss during the day, calculate to miss each night.

The year the sinkhole took the town fountain, we had to use two good sized diesel pickup trucks to wrench the fountain out, reconnect it, pay a crew of two for a day to get it going again on the restored stretch of flat it had months earlier been but a mildly pristine landmark on.

But that was happy past years. This year, like every year, the holes came in, starting in stray places and odd lots, but according to the usual general pattern. Locals informed each other of the arrivals when those arrivals were a bit out of the year to year norm, or in places where the newly settled hole might cause a tangle. People noted the new arrivals, moved on. Nothing unusual. The annual migration. Every year coming and going, coming and going. Just a part of our town.

Within the first month, most of the holes had settled in. We knew we would have to navigate around all the resting holes, maybe brace structures where a hole wedged itself against a foundation, perhaps accept the loss of a ridge of roses to a surly depression. We shrugged. Two months, and they would be migrating again. Minor repairs, minor damage, flat land until the next migration.

This time, after two months of waiting, we were expecting, as always, someone to pop into the Bar and Grill, or lean over their grocery cart at the discount food-a-rama, and say, "You know that hole that I've been saying takes a chunk out of my tomato patch – well, it left this morning. I still see a lot of holes around town, but I am sure glad that one is gone. I might get three more tomato plants in that garden now, have enough tomatoes eventually to surprise the neighbors." And the silent listener would nod and make note to check on the three or four holes most bedeviling his or her progress, hoping those had been among the early migrators.

Not this year, though. People kept waiting for that first testimony of migration. And waiting. Two weeks past the usual start of the migration and no one tauntingly revealed that any hole they knew of had moved on, retired to wherever the holes go after they leave us. Not a single report of the migration out beginning. People began to look at the holes about their living spaces or common travels and think, "Why don't you be first?"

It was a month past the magic moment when the last of the holes would be likely gone, and yet the holes were as numerous as at the peak of their common residency. Theories began to emerge. We had never asked where the holes go, where they came from, whether they went back to where they originated, or on to some place waiting farther on. Could it be that something was blocking them? Could some seasonal home, or some migratory resting place in between, suddenly have become unavailable? Had our rotation in crops, or reshaping the lands, the new strip mall just past the go-cart track, somehow changed our profile to make the holes more comfortable here past their usual season? Or perhaps worse, they had been sapped of their need to migrate, their desire to leave us for elsewhere.

Two months into the time when there should be no holes, we considered demographics, chemistry, news of changes in the counties around us. Reason, reason, reason. Weather, perhaps. An increase in car traffic. All of our answers were maybe, perhaps, could be, possibly, I'd suspect.

This morning, though, Ned, who had been first mock complaining and then actually complaining about a hole at the end of his ten-year-old driveway, went into the hardware store for a bag of off-brand cement mix. Nobody thought anything of it at first. Ned gets funny ideas, and you never know what he is going to find interesting at the hardware store. What might Ned want with cement mix is none of our care.

Then we thought: that driveway is cement; Ned has been working himself up, complaining he has to drive ghoulishly over into his yard to miss that uncaring hole and the grass on that side of the driveway is getting to look less jubilant than the grass everywhere else in his yard. Ned loves his yard. Seeds and weeds, fertilizes, picks up the dog litter. Gets a new lawnmower every ten years whether he needs it or not.

Between many lackluster tellings, several overly calibrated supposi-tions, clipped conclusions - passed through many small crowd institutions and third hand embellishments - an unholy idea came to shine within a critical mass of us: Ned is going to fill that hole.

That would be novel. That would be an experiment against com-monly accepted practice. Year after year we have waited for the holes to move on, expected them to be a resident nuisance for a few months, migrate to wherever they go for the next season. We had already considered trying to map out where they are supposed to go, to more closely inspect the holes to see if this year there were some deformity or rot that kept them in place. Perhaps to measure and catalog to see if some statistic leapt out of the dark and solved the conundrum. But to fill one in: what would that do?

So, faster than opinion can form and demonically branch out, a group of us heads over to Ned's place. A few of us want to see if he is planning to fill the hole, or if he has some other more innocent use for concrete mix. Others have made up their minds and plan, through reason or civic pride, to stop him, ensure without proof that fill in the hole and it will never migrate. Others just want to see what the outcome might be if he actually tried to fill the hole – a hole forced out, a hole locked out of migration, a hole by the same volume expanded, or a hole gone?

We gather in mixed groups, each with our own mission kept close and secret, and take four cars over to Ned's, saying little over the brief hole-dodging ride, parking just down the way from where Ned's driveway dumps into the lane-and-a-half ordinary town street.

There is Ned, actually standing in the street, looking down into the hole, the empty bag of concrete mix, a bucket and hand shovel on the driveway beside the hole.

Or is it still a hole? Or is it now something else, something trapped, something angry, something evolved, or something gone? If Ned would move just a bit out of the way, left or right, we jury of concern could see.

THE PUBLIC DECENCY

The question again is whether the tank should be bigger. It should not be simply round, but should have at least one alcove, and perhaps two. It should be deeper at one end than at the other. There should be shade let languorously out, and natural shade at that – an outcropping, or a tree. And the water must move: it must stir, play and get occasionally agitated.

Not everyone agrees. Some believe it is fine just as it is. Some actually believe it is better as it is than it would be if we did fund and commission all the discussed improvements. It now is little more than a concrete cylinder, with thumping glass making up two thirds of the walls: a tube of water in the middle of a building that would fit into any industrial section of any port city in any nation. The walls are even painted gray.

I, like a lot of our citizens, think we can do better. We have a civic history of respect in how we use the sea. We are a people of cargo, of easy transportation, of flooding, of storm survival. We are a people of bridges and boardwalks and fresh seafood. We are a people of the screw and the rudder. We decorate our homes and yards with oars and oar locks and anchors and anchor chain; and even cheap dives - serving unripe beer, and fifty-year-old bleached easy one-night-stands in overstuffed patent leather pants - have ships' wheels behind their salt leaning bars.

The council meeting will go as always, with the same advocates lining up on the same side, and the new faces on the council having already been lobbied insensitive by the returning incumbents, and everything settled before the public is let into the hall.

The night before this question is on the docket, I go down to the tank, let myself in with my janitor's key, neatly fold and press my clothes onto the raised viewing platform, and quietly slip feet-first into the unfrenzied water. Even though she has seen me drop into her water a dozen times, she still shies to the opposite side of the tank, curls herself as flat as she can against the glass. I bob along the surface, and dive only rarely, proving to her my limitations; and soon she is confident enough to swim under me, to pass around me barely beyond arm's length. The silvery flash of her I catch with the soil-mated back of my eye as she darts close enough to see me in full detail, then retreats when I look directly at her. When I see her wiggle so easily in the cured water, lithe, and bent angelically around the bubbles she makes, I know she can remember the open ocean, remember a time when locomotion could be a straight line, with a varying seascape, a world of unbroken waters to pass through; and perhaps companions, perhaps even live prey.

The next day it is money for pot holes, versus a new tank; money for the high school football team, versus a new tank; repainting the municipal parking lot lines, versus a new tank; lamentation about the reduction in revenue from parking tickets last quarter; and how the real estate tax impacts the bad side of everyone. It is all about how the tank has served us well so far, and is not in need of repair: not nearly in need of repair, yet. It functions. It holds water. It holds our city's symbol.

Unexpectedly, a citizen says perhaps we have kept our mascot long enough. He stands with his hands in his oversized pockets, head held mildly up in expectation. He says that perhaps the tank itself is past its use. His unwarranted hair leaves a ringlet of itself resting on his forehead. He exposes that maintenance of that tank alone must place a penny on everyone's property tax. Perhaps she should be put at the mouth of the river, given back to the elements where she was discovered, and allowed to fend naturally for herself. Now that the novelty has grown thin, and the tourist do not think she is as cute and cathartic as once she was - or once they thought - why would we put so much of our limited resources into that same unchallenging tank, that same once small mermaid, now grown into nearly full maturity. What bleeds out in the cost-benefit analysis?

And so the argument goes, and pot holes win. Yet, there is one resolution. She is older now. Her ballast is drawing more trips from the junior high classes. The boys make gestures of size when they think adults are not looking, hold both palms out in front of themselves like talons, and imagine. Some families avoid the show altogether. So she must now be taught the concept of modesty, taught to wear a thrift store bikini top, or a wet suit tunic: some configuration that brings back a level of public decency. The council will set aside a bit of money. The curator of this small, one exhibit aquarium will teach her how to wear it.

It is a cowardly way of making a point - of agreeing, if only in principle, with the disagreeable.

The paper-loving curator, small and more like a goldfish than a kraken, might fumble with the clothing: hold it at arm's length, sighting through to the mission behind in the tank, to see if it will do the job. He might stand sideways, with the clothing against his own chest, and compare the tool to the object, estimate the best path to utility. He might unwillingly try to imagine how he could do this civic task with but two fingers of each of his hands.

With the doors locked and no one to enjoy the show, he might slip the bra on himself, point to where it should be fastened, to what it should cover. He might smile broadly to indicate his joy at seeing it on himself, and hope that she would so want to please him that she will somehow manage to slip into it, happy ingénue, just as he has dryly illustrated.

But I know that it will be I who must teach her: I, the father of each of her failings. And it is I who must one day take her to the mouth of the river, to swim with her but ten yards towards the ocean and cruelly attempt to instill in her this one thought which fiercely I have been thinking at her all the days of my janitorial supervision - as though my thoughts were more sensible to her than my arid and unintelligible words: half-woman, half-fish, or municipal novelty beyond its time: choose. Choose.

LOVER'S ART

I have watched her now for many long-studded weeks. I think she knows.

I lurk about the edges of the vast field in which she trades. I watch her work the crisscross of lines, comfortable in the slack line between poles, reaching up to the full length of her body where the lines are anchored, drawing herself sometimes on toes: arm creeping longer than I think it will go, her clothes surging up with her, and a slim country of ankle showing quizzically between the hem of her skirt and the roughness of her shoes. Here, at the poles, she slips her sandpaper onto two fingers, sands in short shafts of movement, quickly in staccato covering bare inches, and having to rise and stretch, then collapse, then rise and stretch again, repeating the agony of her being barely long enough over and over.

With the slack lengths of line, away from the clotheslines' end points, she can fold the sandpaper in the flat of her hand, wrap it fully around the line, sand in vigorous long armed dirges, her hand barely above her head. Along these sections, she does not have to stop and stretch and relax and re-adjust her joints and muscles as much as at the ends. Here, she is more eloquent, more fluid, more the ethos of what anyone would expect of a clothesline sander.

Yet, I long to catch her at the ends of the lines – perhaps less graceful, perhaps more a bundle of uncooperating parts that yet holds together and does the job she has shown up to do. It is the striving I long for, the effort. She is, in her difficulty, an opportunity to observe the depth of details necessary to achieve even the clear ordinary.

For half a day, I watch her move along the myriad lines, myself slipping from half-hearted hiding space to half-discovered hiding place, surely by now a known spectator, observed in cheering her every extraordinary move.

At the last, I reluctantly scurry to work, turning back to catch a last fulfilling glimpse as often as is practical to reluctant locomotion.

It has taken me a long time to work up the courage to imagine and then execute a plan to win her. What, ordinarily, would she have to do with someone like me – me, a simple cattle tuner? A workman who moves from farm to farm, tuning other herders' cattle, pocketing my small wage and skittering back to my simple two-room darkening apartment. But, to be worthy of her, I have stirred myself to go farther, to be more, to grow into the range of weeds and notions.

Not that a cattle tuner is of no value. One cow is not much for a family. If the family has two or more, those cattle must be tuned – otherwise, the springing dis-harmonics of the untuned cattle will curdle the milk, malign the cheese, grow gristle in the meet. Cattle in commercial numbers can be even more of a liability if left untuned. What I do has value. Because of tuners like me, families can have two or three or more cattle, industrial cattle employment becomes possible: the bovine arts and products are made more refined, less unruly, predictably more palatable. I make no apologies for my profession. I am an enabler.

A cattle tuner and a clothesline sander could together make a livable wage, one day afford a simple house, raise a stunted family, purchase their small cruet of happiness. But she deserves more. She should have a home of two-stories, her own field of clotheslines, perhaps a barn with navigable cattle. She should have leisure and lace, art and abundance. She should glow with the happiness of the perniciously idle.

So, I have in my own length, learned the weight of mallets; learned the forte strike, the subtle streaking vibration, pacing and the languishing spirits of the notes. I have learned that to hold the mallet tightly is an entirely different sound than to hold the mallet like water, or like the impenetrable head of a child. I have seen what a mystical plot music is. I have learned how to keep the cattle steady, to calm them into compliance, to understand when they no longer think what is being done to them is art. I have taken on a subtlety not rewarded in a cattle tuner, but required of a performer.

And I challenged the Guild for my license. I endured their laughter as they considered that an autodidact, someone not drawn through the crucible of apprenticeship, would challenge for the right to draw music from the cattle he himself has tuned. A man originally only of tuning forks and joint adjustments, shortened horns and bobbed tails. A man of shears and trusses. A workman. Someone whose hands would be lead and wicker against the magical mallets of a trained artist. An honorable man, perhaps; a citizen equal before the law - but not one that might summon wizardry with wood and hide.

Yet they had to yield. Mystified by what I could accomplish for love, their mouths slipped open; stunned, they leaned forward against their collective bench, and their ears piercingly turned greedy. They adjusted their collars and reshuffled their feet. They held their hands unready. An hour they debated, but in the end the question was simply how could one achieve so much in so little time with so little encouragement, and not whether the product was sufficient. No, it was understood as sufficient from the start: the music shouldered its instrument, and I was quietly handed my license.

I will stand in the morning with my borrowed cattle, my small herd tuned and arrayed to become a symphony. I will show my reaching love that I have left the practical and commercial necessity of tuning cattle, instead claiming the advanced stage of playing finely calibrated cattle as art. I will explain that, while these cattle are merely borrowed from my tuning customers, when I advertise my musical intentions, I will be able to collect my own herd; I will be able to be an independent artist. I will play in elite barns, in town-square concerts, in open fields honored to be so used. I will start with just a few cattle, but – all for her, my clothesline sander – I will expand my herd, growing my repertoire, being ever able to play more music, please more aficionados, make ever more in fees and tribute.

I imagine her beginning her day, sure I am watching from some thatch or half-fallen in out-building. She will be creasing the sheaf of sandpaper she expects to use during that day, folding the resistance out of it, making it kind for her hand. She will rub the small of her back, and regard where last she left off sanding, and the length of line soon to be addressed.

I will play those ruled cattle, and her love will be shyly seduced with the appreciation of my bovine symphony. At first, she will not know the source of the music, my cattle almost hidden in the rough grass at the edge of the clothesline field. She will stop in mid-reach, her head drifting in circles, her eyes focused to the far and not the near: the line to be sanded forgotten, her hand still burdened with the sandpaper, her ears and then her eyes, pulled to me. With all binary dreams of sanding forgotten, she will delicately hear my proposal, focus at last on me and in wonder recognize he who once was a workman in terrible love, but who now is a thunderously gossamer artist waiting to be rudely loved.

IN SYMPATHY

I have always believed the rumors. I have talked to half a dozen people who have seen it themselves. Nash says he took a shot at it. I've been hunting with Nash often enough to know he shoots at loose shadows and misses even those, but I'll take his word on this one. Anything could be in the woods and swamps that swallow up our little bit of tenuous civilization. There are places in the swamp that not even the dumbest of hunters or backwoodsman stumble, drunk or sober, onto. Who knows what mightily mysterious thing could be living out there?

Where the legend is centered, in location, is generally called Sympathy. Unincorporated. No sign. Maybe the name is just a local custom. Maybe someone named Sympathy once lived there. Doesn't matter. For the longest time there were just three houses there, dropped casually on the land as though out of a passing vast cargo plane: one with a school bus out back that sometimes squatters would claim: squatters who sometimes became quite friendly and did odd-jobs for the real owners. Day traffic on the two-lane road runs from the cities north to the beaches south, sometimes turned out to be a reason for locked back doors and an eventual shot over the hood of the bus. Most people catch it only in the rear-view mirror. Alongside the road, the swamp runs mostly up to the pavement, except for the huge drainage ditch. It's been said there are alligators in that ditch. I've never seen any, never looked for any, and I'm not pressing my luck.

In Sympathy, those three small-plot farmers have built the land up, can actually create dust with a tractor. In summer, they put out a roadside stand and sell produce to the tourists. Cars park in their front yards or precariously on the tilted strip of ragged wild grass between the drainage ditch and the pavement: depending upon how the car is tilted and the recent rains, all those infesting the car have to get out of the same side of the vehicle.

The swamps, however, grow strong right up to the last of the tilled sections. The residents spend part of each week beating the wilderness back. Ten feet into the bramble, if you are not familiar with the land, you could be lost until next season.

I do not know why it was particularly there, in Sympathy, that the Swamp Man was rumored to stay. People say it has a long legend, but you only hear that from people alive today, and they can be mistaken or given to embellishment. Embellishment or not, what matters is what people still here, with the power to act in the present day, believe – and enough think there is sufficient collectable substance to the story for it to stick. We've got a lot of dark to fill around here.

Pretty much the description of the Swamp Man matches those of any of the nation's other anthropomorphic monsters: Bigfoot, Boggy Creek Monster, Old Stinky, Grassman - all the other shadow monsters seen in unabridged half looks. Seven feet tall, upright like a man, size seventeen feet, shaggy, smelly. Given to low growls which everyone who has heard them swears is not the wind. Hard to see for something that size.

Every time a raccoon gets into someone's trash, it gets blamed on the Swamp Man. Girls, who have gotten a little too much on track with their dates' plans in a car parked at the edge of the woods, have backed up by hearing the Swamp Man breathing about the car. Boys, who didn't get as far along as they would like to be bragging to their friends about the next day, say the Swamp Man showed up just as they were rounding Third and were steaming octopus-like Home: thud went a paw on the car and the moment was gone. Drivers on the road who zigged when they should have zagged swore they did so to miss the Swamp Man racing to his own dark decisions between both far sides of the road.

More fun to think it true than not. Better to be put out by a monster than to strike out on your own. If he is not real, at least he is convenient.

At some point, it became fashionable to go looking for the Swamp Man. Friends would gather their shotguns and head for Sympathy: a cooler of beer, a box of shells. You had to park alongside the road, far enough down from the houses that you would not shoot anyone accidentally, sitting angled just towards the ditch so as to be out of the road, and just towards the road so as not to slide into the ditch.

Many a detail about the Swamp Man grew out of coolers going nearly empty; and many a cloud, if it were hanging a little low, was well seeded with poorly aimed buckshot.

The county police asked us to be a little less liberal with our shotguns, as we would often stay close to the road and the farmers' houses and our vehicles where the coolers yowled; so the trip to see the Swamp Man was determined to settle on the coolers of beer, not the opportunity to see if the rumored monster was immune to buckshot.

Someone a little later, just past the last farm on the left, put in a gas station/convenience store, with an asphalt parking lot – betting on the beach tourist traffic going by and maybe a little on the Swamp Man interest — and they would let cars stay in the lot an hour or two if someone in the car bought gas or beer or some trinket at the store. All over-priced, but where else did we have to go?

A six pack doesn't last long enough to get warm, so suddenly a cooler was no longer required. The convenience store stocked everyone's favorite. The whole Swamp Man phenomenon moved to the back corner of that parking lot, and boys in twos and threes would head there mid-evenings to search from their cars for the Swamp Man, or at least take advantage of the store's desk clerk's liberal ID policy.

They renamed the store "Swamp Man Convenience", and many wondered why the owners did not start with that name. Some nights the store was slinging self-service gas and rock-solid national brand beer nearly as fast as if it were located twelve miles up at the tourist strip that hugs the beach like a cheap fake-fur stole.

I kept waiting for the run to peter out, for Swamp Man to become again something parents might trot out to scare children, teens might reference to get closer to their dates - but there was a simplicity, and even an authenticity, about the Swamp Man legend that gave it dark-blue momentum. Couples would go out to catch the Swamp Man, sit half the night at the dark end of the store's sufficiently barely-lit lot, illuminating the near woods with flashlight, illuminating the rocking cars three empty parking places over where you could catch now and again a body part or head thrust up to window level, perfectly entertained for only the cost of batteries, a six pack, and, if luck were with them, one ill-fitting condom.

It was inevitable: the store began to sell Swamp Man memorabilia.

Then, bracketing the residents, someone plowed out, at the other end of Sympathy, space for the Swamp Man Lounge. Just a shack with a small grill, cooler and a dancer runway. When it finally opened, featuring over-priced burgers and over-priced beer and three short sets of topless entertainment from nine to midnight, the Swamp Man story moved again, coming to rest just out of view off the back corner of the lounge's back parking lot. For a legend, he was fairly particularly about where you should go to get a glimpse of him. There were some who were loyal to the convenience store, but the legal age crowd gravitated to the lounge. And it was assumed Swamp Man was of legal age, and would probably slink down to the lounge end of the developing commerce strip.

Laugh at the idea of Swamp Man if you will, but the Swamp Man convenience employs four locals; the Swamp Man Lounge hired another six, and it is rumored that when the lounge's current contract for dancers expires, they might freelance local talent. All the wives know where their husbands are when they say they are going out to hunt the Swamp Man. And, if Nelly's saucy cousin achieves a performance contract with the lounge, everyone will soon know if the plus-size rumors about her are true, too.

Given that Swamp Man is still out there, I wonder what he thinks of all the commerce and commotion. I suspect all the extra trash and the abandoned half-empty beers in the lounge and convenience store parking lots probably make his night-stalking a little less important, a little more dangerous for him — and his need to pop out at the unsuspecting has probably slipped behind his need to understand how to pop open a half lazily locked dumpster. All creatures get a little lazy when the environment changes for the easier.

But if he is still out there, I bet it is not long before he curls at a flashy trot, accidentally or with some resurrected purpose, across the lounge's dead-end parking lot, exposes himself to a closing-time dribble of stupefied customers who might not believe, who might be thinking all this Swamp Man hype is good local color for the tourists. Swamp Man, with his almost human gait, showing to all in Sympathy that at least he believes in himself.

Heck, I'm rooting for him. Sure, Swamp Man lives! I'm rooting for all of us.

ALSO BY KEN POYNER:

Constant Animals, brief fictions

Avenging Cartography, brief fictions

The Revenge of the House Hurlers, brief fictions

Victims of a Failed Civics, speculative poetry

The Book of Robot, speculative poetry